THE GAMES PEOPLE PLAY

DI SARA RAMSEY
BOOK TWENTY-ONE

M A COMLEY

For Mum, you never let me down, thank you for giving me the tools and the backing to begin this incredible journey.

Miss you every minute of every day, you truly were a Mum in a million. My heart, my soul.

ACKNOWLEDGMENTS

Special thanks as always go to @studioenp for their superb cover design expertise.

My heartfelt thanks go to my wonderful editor Emmy, and my proofreaders Joseph and Barbara for spotting all the lingering nits.

Thank you also to my amazing ARC Group who help to keep me sane during this process.

To Mary, gone, but never forgotten. I hope you found the peace you were searching for my dear friend. I miss you each and every day.

ALSO BY M A COMLEY

Seeking Justice (a 15,000 word novella)

Caring For Justice (a 24,000 word novella)

Savage Justice (a 17,000 word novella)

Justice at Christmas #2 (a 15,000 word novella)

Gone in Seconds (Justice Again series #1)

Ultimate Dilemma (Justice Again series #2)

Shot of Silence (Justice Again series #3)

Taste of Fury (Justice Again series #4)

Crying Shame (Justice Again series #5)

See No Evil (Justice Again #6)

To Die For (DI Sam Cobbs #1)

To Silence Them (DI Sam Cobbs #2)

To Make Them Pay (DI Sam Cobbs #3)

To Prove Fatal (DI Sam Cobbs #4)

To Condemn Them (DI Sam Cobbs #5)

To Punish Them (DI Sam Cobbs #6)

To Entice Them (DI Sam Cobbs #7)

To Control Them (DI Sam Cobbs #8)

To Endanger Lives (DI Sam Cobbs #9)

To Hold Responsible (DI Sam Cobbs #10)

To Catch a Killer (DI Sam Cobbs #11)

Forever Watching You (DI Miranda Carr thriller)

Wrong Place (DI Sally Parker thriller #1)

No Hiding Place (DI Sally Parker thriller #2)

Cold Case (DI Sally Parker thriller#3)

Deadly Encounter (DI Sally Parker thriller #4)

Lost Innocence (DI Sally Parker thriller #5)

Goodbye My Precious Child (DI Sally Parker #6)

Merry Widow (A Lorne Simpkins short story)

It's A Dog's Life (A Lorne Simpkins short story)

A Time To Heal (A Sweet Romance)

A Time For Change (A Sweet Romance)

High Spirits

The Temptation series (Romantic Suspense/New Adult Novellas)

Past Temptation

Lost Temptation

Clever Deception (co-written by Linda S Prather)

Tragic Deception (co-written by Linda S Prather)

Sinful Deception (co-written by Linda S Prather)

PROLOGUE

 *aturday*

THE WIND HOWLED AROUND the corner of the building. Adam's muscles were tense and achy after his exertions at the gym. He'd completed a full circuit of the equipment in a competition with his mate, Stefan, and he was now suffering as a result. Legs like jelly, barely able to keep him upright. He kicked himself for not bringing the car tonight. His girl-friend, Elly, had warned him that the weather was going to be turning autumnal soon. Why hadn't he listened to her?

Because I always know best or I think I do. No one likes a smart arse. I think I'm going to learn that the hard way. I know, I'll pick up a bottle of wine from the off-licence on the way to make it up to Elly, or to drown my sorrows after pushing myself to the limits... whatever takes my fancy when I get back home.

He kicked out at a medium-sized stone on the pavement. It spun off at an angle, hit the wall and came back to whack him on the ankle. "Jesus, just my luck. Can this night get any worse? Don't ask, it's brewing up for a downpour, and I'm still ten minutes from home. I'd better up my pace," he grumbled, aware that no one else was around who might think he had lost his marbles, talking to himself.

Ahead of him, a white van pulled up. He was on the edge of the city, at Eign Hill, close to the vet's practice where he worked six days a week, sometimes seven, if needed. He dipped his head as another gust of wind battered him. This time it was accompanied by a ferocious bout of rain. He upped his pace. With his head bowed low, he hadn't noticed the door of the van spring open until he ran into it.

"Shit, sorry. That'll teach me to look where I'm going."

A bloke in his thirties, a few inches taller than Adam, jumped out of the van and crossed his arms in front of him. "You wanna watch where you're going, mate. You nearly took my door off its hinges."

"Yeah, let's blame the weather, shall we?" Adam smiled at the man who shook his head.

"It won't wash with me, moron. You're gonna pay for not watching where you're going."

Adam hitched his sports holdall on his right shoulder and raised his hands again. "Sorry, pal. I don't want any aggro. All I need to do is be on my way. It's been a long day, and I'm in dire need of some grub."

"Here, let me take your bag, and we'll give you a lift."

"Nah, you're all right, but thanks for the offer."

"I said, get in the fucking van." The man's sinister tone carried on the wind.

Adam took a step backwards, but the man reached out a hand and grabbed him by the throat. The movement was abrupt, and Adam could do little to get away from this angry stranger. The man's strength overwhelmed him, and within seconds he found himself being bundled in through the side door of the van, the man's frame sitting on top of him, crushing his arms.

"Drive," his kidnapper shouted, and the van sped away, spinning its wheels.

"What are you doing? Get off me. I demand to know what you're going to do with me!" Adam shouted. A sense of doom swept over him. He was pretty sure this thug had no intention of giving him any answers. He refused to let up and bombarded his abductor with yet more questions, until the goon had finally had enough and rammed a piece of cloth into his mouth.

"Thank fuck for that, his shitting voice was pounding my ears," the driver called over his shoulder with a laugh.

Adam's fear hit a new level. It was obvious that neither of the men had any intention of easing up on him. *What the fuck? I don't recognise either of them. Why haven't they got their faces covered? That can only mean one thing, can't it? They're going to do away with me.* That left him one option: to sit still and do all he could to summon up the strength to fight for his life if it came to it.

He watched the sights of Hereford city centre whizz past through the windscreen until there were no buildings of interest to highlight the route they were taking. All he knew was they had crossed the river and had driven past Asda at the bottom of the hill. Where they had gone from there was beyond him. He wasn't as familiar with the roads on this side of the city when he worked and lived on the opposite side.

The van suddenly jerked to a halt, sending the prick, who had him pinned down, flying into the back of the driver's seat. "You frigging clown, you could have warned me you were going to slam on the brakes."

"Sorry, I didn't think. In fact, I nearly drove past this shit-hole and only recognised the crumbling wall at the side," the driver retorted harshly. "So wind your sodding neck in. Are you ready to unload the cargo?"

"Yep. You hop out. Check the coast is clear. We'll get him in the house swiftly."

"I'm up for that. Let's go."

Adam prepared himself as much as he could. He'd go down fighting if that's what these two idiots wanted, or would he? Did he have it in him to take on the pair of them?

The side door slid open. The goon on top of him slithered off but wrapped his arms around Adam's torso and forced him out of the van. Adam attempted to cry out, but the cloth filling his mouth was successful in scuppering his efforts.

Shit! What can I do now? I'm screwed, well and truly.

Between them, the two men shunted him up a garden path that led to what had to be one of the worst houses in the city. The driver used a key to unlock a padlock on the front door, and within seconds they were inside the musty-smelling, damp interior. He tried to complain but received several jabs to the stomach from the bloke who had initially spoken to and then abducted him.

"Shut up. We'll tell you when you can speak."

An apology circulated Adam's mind but never reached his lips. He thought better of it, in case his audacity caused him yet more trouble. He was forced to ascend the staircase that creaked and groaned under the weight of the three of them.

"These have almost had it. Maybe we should use one of the rooms downstairs instead, you know, for when we collect the others," the driver said.

"Good point. We'll use the bedroom for now, get him settled, and then sort out which room to utilise downstairs for our needs."

One of the men removed the cloth from Adam's mouth and pushed him into a room which contained a soiled mattress lying on the floor. The mattress matched the rest of the property in that it had seen better days. Again, Adam couldn't prevent his enquiring mind from wondering what was about to happen to him. He studied each of the men in turn, but there wasn't a glimmer of recognition there. Without them telling him what this abduction was all about, there was no way of him knowing if he had wronged them in any way, and he couldn't come right out and ask them, either.

The man kicked out, whipping Adam's legs from under him. He landed on the mattress with a thud. It was thin, and the springs were prominent, poking him in the arse. Instead of inserting the cloth again, the goon tore off a length of gaffer tape and stretched it across his mouth. Adam did his best to pounce on the opportunity to speak, but the manoeuvre was carried out succinctly and with precision.

One of them tied his feet and the other kept him subdued with a knife at his throat, then the two men left him and went back downstairs, but not before they searched his clothes for any sharp objects or a possible mobile. He was aware he'd been parted from his bag that was still in the back of the van, along with his phone.

Jesus, I really am up shit creek here. What the fuck are they intending to do with me? Why are they holding me in this shithole? Elly, please, go to the police and report me missing. Don't delay, it could be a matter of life or death... mine!

HE SLEPT in fits and spurts throughout the night, listening for any possible movements going on in the house, unaware if he was sharing it with anyone else. The opportunity to call out had been stolen from him. The men had mentioned 'the others'. Did that mean he was the first of many? Were there other people already here, in another room? He had hundreds of similar questions running through his head; he

5

was generally the inquisitive sort, but the most prominent one of all was: why? Why the fuck was this happening to him? He didn't have the foggiest idea why someone would have the desire to kidnap him and keep him in a hellhole like this, with no food or water to see him through the night, not that he would be able to eat or drink with his mouth taped up. Why?

The two men showed up the next morning with a burger and a milkshake. He detested anything served from the well-known outlet. The driver made a point of saying that there was no alternative on offer and he would starve if he didn't eat it. After he'd consumed the lump of grease and washed it down with the sickly shake, yet another piece of tape was slapped over his mouth and the men disappeared once more.

He was left alone until the day turned into night, then the men returned, this time with a sandwich and a can of pop. The driver removed the tape.

"I don't want to hear you complaining. If you do, you go without food and drink for the foreseeable, got that?"

Adam nodded. And tore open the sandwich which was at least a couple of days old, not that he cared. It was a hundred times better than the greasy burger that had been forced upon him earlier that day. He washed it down with the can of Coke and rubbed at his lips, enjoying the freedom from the tape, but it didn't last long. "Please, you don't need to put that on me. I promise not to shout out if you leave me here."

His comment was met with a fist in the face before a piece of fresh tape was stretched over his mouth. His jaw throbbed, and he couldn't open and close it to gain any relief. He watched the men leave the room, and his heart sank at having to spend another night on the uncomfortable mattress. His captors hadn't even allowed him the dignity of going to the toilet since he'd been abducted. His personal hygiene long forgotten, the smell emanating from his jogging pants could only be described as putrid. He tried his best to ignore it but struggled. He found the urge to vomit overwhelming, aware that if he did, the consequences would be devastating. So, he kept swallowing down the bile burning his throat and blocked out his humiliation by constantly thinking of happier times with Elly and his friends. The holidays they had gone on over the past few years, to Mexico and Antigua, which had been his personal favourite. Swimming in a blue lagoon they had stumbled across on one of their adventures. Somehow, he managed to succumb to sleep, his mind with Elly, drifting on a boat across the lagoon, surrounded by all of his friends and family, the ones who meant so much to him. Secretly, he prayed as well, that God would take him while he slept. It was hard quashing the ominous feeling surging through him, that the end was nigh.

THE FOLLOWING day consisted of much the same, except the kidnappers gave him a pasty for breakfast. The day dragged by, minute by minute, hour by hour. They still hadn't shown him any decency by allowing him to use the loo. He was tired of restraining his bodily function. He could feel the warmth of the shit in his pants turn to a squishy mess every time he chose to change position and turn over. Someone would pay for degrading him like this, when the time came, if he got out of this situation alive, which was an enormous *if* in his eyes.

As dusk descended and the men hadn't shown up with any further offerings of food, he resigned himself to being hungry all night and forced any thoughts of savoury or sweet snacks from his mind. Until darkness filled the room and movement sounded downstairs. Someone was creeping around down there. Did he have the guts to try and grab their attention? What if it turned out to be the terrible twosome, playing with him, seeing what he got up to in their

7

absence? He decided the best option would be to remain still, his ear cocked, straining to listen.

After a few moments, the door to the bedroom burst open, and two masked figures entered. His fear increased and teetered on the edge of an impending abyss. Behind the tape he shouted, "No, don't. You have to help me. Please, they might come back at any moment. Help me escape, I've got money in the bank."

The two masked intruders froze for a second or two, obviously understanding snippets of what he'd said. By this time, they had hoisted him to his feet, one man standing on either side of him. They were both taller than Adam, and his head swivelled from one to the other. Trepidation, and even hope, grew within.

He repeated the words a second time. "I have money."

"Got an envelope or a scrap of paper on you?" one of the men asked the other.

"What am I? A walking stationery cupboard?"

"Don't fucking talk to me like that, I only asked." The goon searched his pocket and found the lid off a cigarette packet lingering at the bottom.

"Shit, I know what's coming next, you'll be wanting a pen now, won't you? Well, I ain't got one. So now what?"

The man stopped and removed a pencil from his sock. "Don't bother, I've got this." He prodded Adam in the gut. "I'm going to take the tape off now. Any funny business, and I'll slit your throat, you hear me?"

Petrified, Adam nodded enthusiastically. The man tutted and tore the tape from his mouth.

"Right, let's have it. Sort code and account number, and what bank is it?"

Adam closed his eyes, imagined his bank details written down in front of him and gave them to the goon who squeezed the information onto the piece of card. "It's the NatWest bank."

"Great. Slap another piece of tape over his mouth to shut the fucker up while I make the transfer."

"What the fuck? How are you going to do that? You need his password to his banking app and do it from there, don't ya?"

"Do I? Fucked if I know, I haven't transferred money before. You know what? I can't be frigging arsed. What's the point anyway? The police will have a paper trail then, won't they? Nah, it's not worth the hassle. I mean, the money would have come in handy but, sooooo not worth it."

"You're right. It's a good job you've got your head screwed on."

"Ain't it just? Let's get out of here."

Both men grabbed Adam's arms and steered him out of the room and down the stairs. They paused at the front door to check the coast was clear and then marched him into the van. Adam thought it was the same van the kidnappers had used to bring him to the location. At that moment, the penny dropped. These were the same fuckers, and they were in the process of moving him to a different location. Why?

Had someone spotted them coming and going from the house and reported them to the police? What's with the ski masks? Why are they disguising their faces now? None of this is making any frigging sense.

The door to the house was secured with the padlock again. They opened the side door of the van, and this time Adam raised his legs, spreading them so they were either side of the doorway. One of the men kicked him up the arse, and the other thumped him in the stomach. His legs dropped to the ground, and he was thrown into the back of the van. One man sat on top of him while the other jumped into the driver's seat, revved the engine then took off.

Shit, where are they taking me? I've fucked things up, playing the big I am, stupid macho man, and where did that fucking get me? Nowhere, that's where. He closed his eyes, hoping his happy thoughts would shroud him and chase away the fear.

"Jesus, he stinks. I reckon he's shat himself," the bloke next to Adam shouted, causing him further humiliation.

The journey turned out to be a fairly long one, or maybe it wasn't and it just felt that way because of the circumstances. Either way, the van drew to a stop, and the man inched himself off Adam.

The driver threw open the side door, and the men stared down at him. Adam strained his neck to see what awaited him behind the driver, but the darkness shielded his view.

"Where are we? What are you going to do with me?" he asked, the tape stifling his words.

"Stop talking and get out of the fucking van, dickhead."

The other man leapt out, and then, together, they latched on to each of Adam's legs and dragged him out of the vehicle.

Adam recognised the parking area. This was a favourite haunt for him and Elly; they enjoyed taking Jasper for a walk through the forest. *Is this place significant?* He couldn't ask, not with his mouth still taped up. Why had they brought him here? It's not like the area was well lit. It consisted of a dense forest with a lake. His fear notched up to yet another level. He searched the men's faces, although the masks were still firmly in place. Their eyes gave nothing away and left him wanting.

"Let's take him into the woods. I know just the spot," the driver said.

Both men laughed. Adam gulped, and they laughed again. The men guided him and set off. He dug his heels in, refused to move, but they laid into him. Punched him in the stomach a few times.

Adam doubled over in pain and shouted, "Why?"

Neither of his abductors responded. They grasped both his arms and continued on their journey, pausing when they came to a small opening surrounded by mature trees. The last time Elly and Adam had been here, he had taken her in his arms and kissed her, long and hard, enjoying the romance of the area. If he survived this encounter, whatever the men had planned for him, he knew he would never see this place in the same light ever again.

"This will do. Have you got it?" the driver asked.

The other man unzipped his jacket and removed a length of rope with a noose on the end. He turned to Adam and smiled.

Adam shook his head and pleaded over and over again until his throat felt raw.

The men ignored him and got to work. The end of the rope was looped over one of the lower branches.

"Is this going to be too low? Maybe that one over there would be better suited for what we have in mind," the driver said.

"Yep, I was about to suggest the same. Come on, get a move on, I sense it's blowing up for rain."

"That's to our advantage, it'll keep the walkers away. Less chance of him being discovered early." The driver moved to within a foot of the selected tree and threw the rope over one of the thicker branches. He tested its strength and when he was satisfied, he approached Adam and draped the noose around his neck while the other goon held him in place.

Despite Adam's attempts to hinder the driver's progress, he failed. Adam closed his eyes, sudden resignation dawning on him that there was no way out of this situation. His life was about to end, and there was nothing he could do about it.

CHAPTER 1

*S*ara felt rested after her week away in The Lakes. She and Mark had ventured north, hired a mobile home and taken Misty, their adorable cat, with them. Their bundle of fluff had enjoyed the attention and her different walks on her harness. All in all, the holiday had been a huge success, but now it was back to work with a bump for both of them. Mark had set off early because he had an emergency operation to perform at seven-thirty that morning.

He'd given her a long, lingering kiss and whispered, "All over too soon, wasn't it?"

"Sadly true. We'll have to go again, maybe in March or April. It's supposed to be beautiful up there in the springtime."

He had smiled. "Something to look forward to, I suppose. Have a good day. I hope you don't have too much paperwork to deal with."

"That makes two of us. I hope the operation goes well. See you later."

Sara was now relaxed, listening to Smooth Radio on her way into the city. She'd forgotten how bad the traffic was at that time of the morning and she could feel her temperature rising through her frustration at the morons daring to be on the road at the same time as her.

After taking a few deep breaths, keen to retain the good mood she had left the house in, she pulled into the station car park and drove into her allotted space. Seconds later, Carla, her long-suffering partner, drew up alongside her.

They smiled and exited their vehicles.

"I'd ask how your holiday went, except it's written all over your face."

"Sorry, the last thing I want to do is rub it in. How did things go around here? Solve any major crimes while I was away?"

"Nope, I think most of the vile criminals took the week off when they heard the great DI Sara Ramsey wasn't around to play ball with them."

Sara laughed. "You reckon?" She pushed open the door to the main entrance.

Jeff Makepeace, the desk sergeant, greeted her with the warmest of smiles. "Here she is, looking fully refreshed and eager for action."

"I am, Jeff. I hope you've kept Carla in line during my time off?"

"I have, ma'am. She's been putty in my hands." He laughed at Carla's mortified expression.

"Believe that and you'll believe anything," Carla mumbled. She punched in her code and opened the door that led them into the inner sanctum.

"It's good to be back," Sara admitted. She climbed the stairs with Carla.

"You'll come back down to earth with a bang once you've tasted your first cup of shitty coffee."

"Great. I was hoping that the DCI had sanctioned a new

coffee machine in my absence. Clearly yet another delusional thought by moi."

"Yeah, I think you're going to need to close your eyes and imagine you're sipping a flat white elsewhere, overlooking a lake with a stunning mountain as a backdrop."

"Now that isn't such a bad idea. I had plenty of inspiration. When are you due to go away?"

"Not for another few weeks."

"And you're going abroad, aren't you?"

"Yes, to Majorca or Mallorca, however you want to say it. First time for me, but Des has been countless times before. He adores it there."

"You'll have a blast. Mum and Dad took us when we were all younger."

"How's your father doing?"

"He's having a fabulous time with his new girlfriend, Margaret. She's so different to Mum; she's definitely keeping him on his toes."

"Ordering him about?"

"I wouldn't put it that way. Hmm... suggesting he should do things a certain way, how's that?"

"Bless him. He's happy, though?"

"Extremely. Hasn't got a minute to himself and is always on the go doing little jobs here and there. I have to say he's thriving on it, so why alter things?"

They reached the landing and entered the incident room.

Sara paused to take in the atmosphere. "I never thought these words would tumble out of my mouth, but I actually missed this place."

"You'll soon change your mind about that when you see the paperwork littering your desk. Coffee?"

Sara groaned. "You told me you would handle it in my absence. Yes, add a little extra sugar, I'll need it, to combat the shock."

"Go through, I'll bring it in."

Sara tentatively took a few steps towards her office. She pushed open the door and gasped. "Jesus, what the fuck, Carla?"

"I know. I can give you a hand. We'll sift through it in no time at all."

"Er… if that's the case then why didn't you sodding well do it last week while I was away?"

"That's only a portion of what I had to deal with, the rest of the team will back me up."

Sara shook her head, entered her office, and her gaze was immediately drawn to the mountains beyond. She had always regarded the Brecon Beacons as her happy place and often went up there for a hike, however, after seeing the sights on offer in The Lakes, her opinion was waning slightly now. Nevertheless, the view did the job of calming her, if only for a moment or two.

Carla joined her, two mugs of coffee in hand. "Want me to help now?"

"Take a seat. You can fill me in while I make a start and put the letters in some semblance of order."

They took a seat. Sara felt at home as soon as she slotted her legs under the desk.

"There's really nothing to tell. I concentrated on getting through this lot—it's not my fault a new pile has been added overnight—while the team concentrated on closing the few open cases we had, you know, paperwork and reports wise."

"That's brilliant news. So you're all up to date out there then?"

"As well as we can be. There's bound to be something head office wants us to amend down the line, there always is."

"And DCI Price left you alone to get on with it?"

"Mostly. She popped in a few times, I think to check that

we weren't slacking. Which we weren't, I can assure you. I went home exhausted most nights, we all did."

"I'm grateful for you filling in and doing your best to keep on top of things, Carla. I'm aware of what a chore that can be at times."

Carla took a sip from her mug. "You're not kidding. At least you had another day to prepare yourself for tackling this lot."

"Yes, having the Bank Holiday added to my time off was an absolute bonus. I didn't plan it that way, I promise."

"Yeah, I believe you."

"How's Des getting on? Is he behaving around the house now? Stumping up with housekeeping money or still taking the piss?"

Carla tutted and rolled her eyes. "No, all is good. We had a heart to heart while you were on your jollies, and he was ashamed I had to point out the error of his ways. He's put extra funds in my account to cover all the bills, which are racking up now that the colder weather is about to hit us."

"Yep, bang goes the summer and cheaper bills, eh? Back to reality with a bang. Hey, at least we're out at work all day, making the most of the heating around here. Can you imagine what it's like being a pensioner, stuck on a fixed income, making the decision to either eat or heat?"

"It doesn't bear thinking about. As long as our families are okay, I can't imagine you allowing your father to go without, just like I wouldn't my parents."

"True enough. Anyway, ploughing on."

Sara sorted the letters into piles, sipping at her extra-sweetened coffee at the same time, ignoring the bitterness of the beans. She handed the easier letters to Carla to deal with and then booted up her computer to find over two hundred emails awaiting her. "Fuck, why do we bother going on holiday if this is what we have to deal with upon our return?"

17

Carla opened her mouth, and Sara raised a hand to stop her from speaking.

"And no, I wasn't having a go at you. I'm aware that you've done your best."

"I still feel like I've let you down. I admit, I didn't get around to answering your emails. I didn't know how to get into your account for one thing."

"Don't worry, it's fine, I'll sort it during the day. Let's deal with this crap first."

The other team members all stuck their heads into the office to welcome her back. After about an hour, Sara relieved Carla of her duties.

Her partner appeared pleased to be dismissed when she breezed out of the room. "Another coffee?"

"Yep, extra-extra sweet this time, sod the calories, needs must."

Carla laughed and left the room. Sara bowed her head, ready to tackle the last pile of dross but was interrupted by the phone moments later.

"Hey, you, back to it. Knee-deep in unwanted paperwork, eh? And no, I don't need a crystal ball to know that."

Sara smiled at her dear friend's quip. "How did you guess? Is this a 'welcome back' call or do you need my expertise somewhere, Lorraine?"

"The latter. Want to join me out at Belmont Country Park ASAP?"

Sara groaned. "If I must. And there was me hoping to ease myself in gently."

"Get away with you, you've had an extra day off, you know the drill of what is expected of you. See you soon."

Sara laughed and ended the call. She collected her jacket from the coat rack and then her partner from the incident room. "Our company is wanted at Belmont Country Park, that's all I know at the moment."

"I swear you attract bad crimes. There must be an alert that goes out in the underground when you return to work."

"You're probably right. I need to stock up on protectives before we head over there."

THE AREA WAS full of tech vans.

"Must be a bad one to have all these in attendance," Carla muttered the second Sara drew up alongside Lorraine's vehicle.

"I can't help you there, Lorraine didn't tell me. Come on, let's get partially togged up."

They pulled on their suits and gloves but left their shoe covers off until they got closer to the actual crime scene.

"What have we got?" Sara asked, perplexed.

"This young man was found hanging from that tree, and no, I don't think it was self-inflicted," Lorraine replied.

"Er... obvious question, why not?"

"Because there are other injuries on his body. Although there wasn't tape over his mouth when we discovered him, there are signs of tape having been used, and this." She held up a slip of paper in a plastic evidence bag.

Sara peered and frowned. "What's that? A suicide note?"

"Far from it. Shall we call it a 'method of kill' note?"

Sara faced her, and her frown deepened. "I'm not with you."

Lorraine heaved out a sigh. "It's a note from the killer, describing in great detail, exactly what happened to him."

"What? Can I see it?"

Lorraine handed the bag to Sara. The note had creases in it where it had been folded in four.

"And it was found in his mouth?" Sara asked, for clarification.

"That's right."

Sara's cheeks puffed out. She read aloud what was written on the note. "Victim one. Kidnap, hold for a few days at the location. Take him out to Belmont Country Park and string him up from one of the trees. Bye-bye, Mr Nice Guy."

Carla let out a low whistle. "What the actual fuck? If that's the case, why remove the tape from his mouth? Wouldn't it have dropped out if he cried out for help?"

"Possibly. Maybe he was already dead. Or perhaps the killer hanged him and then lowered his body again to shove the note inside," Sara said.

"Either way," Lorraine added, "I think we're dealing with a sick fucker and, if you believe what they wrote on the note, there are more victims to follow."

"Fuck," Sara said, "that clue passed me by for a second or two. What the hell is going on here? Any ID found on the body?"

"Nothing. No vehicle dumped here. Nothing. You're up against it from the outset."

"Great. I'm going to need to take a photo, is that okay?" Sara checked with Lorraine.

"Go for it."

Sara took a few steps closer to the victim and withdrew her phone from her pocket. "Who found him and when?"

"A jogger. He was in a rush to get to work, he's a solicitor. He left his card, said he'll be in the office all morning and has to be in court this afternoon."

Lorraine handed Sara a business card.

"Thanks, Lorraine. We'll check in with him. Anything else here? No other witnesses? No vehicles seen near the scene? Anything at all for us to cling on to?"

"Nothing. Except back where the cars are parked. The killer must have driven him here, hoisted him up and buggered off. How long that process took to carry out is anyone's guess. Whether he was dead already when he got here or was marched through the woods to the kill site, again, is anyone's guess at this point, until the PM has been completed."

"Bugger, too many variables, and the likelihood of you obtaining any evidence from the car park which is probably used regularly by the locals, is what? Negligible?"

"Obviously we'll do our very best for you but, yeah, I wouldn't hold out much hope on that front if I were you."

"What sort of injuries or bruises has he got?"

They crouched beside the body, and Lorraine lifted the victim's sports top.

"Bruises to the stomach. Maybe he was kept in check with a few sharp digs with someone's fingers." Lorraine demonstrated butting her fingertips into the palm of her other hand.

"Possibly. Anything else?"

"Not yet, I've got a feeling a lot of other injuries will come to light during the PM which I will be carrying out this afternoon."

"Great. I'll be expecting your report either tonight or tomorrow then?"

"Wishful thinking on your part. It depends on how long we hang around here," Lorraine confirmed.

"But you're going to do your best for us, aren't you?"

Lorraine narrowed her eyes. "Don't I always?"

"All right, you've got me there. Can we have a walk around the area? I just need to get a feel for things before we head off and speak with the witness."

"Go for it, just don't get in our way."

Sara grinned at her pathologist friend. "As if we would."

Sara and Carla set off, away from the crime scene.

"What are you thinking?" Carla asked.

"I'm not, not really. Something doesn't feel right, though."

"In what respect?"

Sara shrugged. "I wish I knew. This place isn't that popular, is it? I mean, it might be with the locals who live within spitting distance of it, but would it be somewhere you choose to come to, given the choice?"

"You're not making any sense. I wouldn't personally come here but even I can tell the car park is well used, judging by how worn down it is."

Sara nodded and stared off into the distance. "I'm just saying it's not usually a likely kill site, is it?"

"How can you say that? Your logic is beyond me at the best of times."

Sara laughed. "Maybe I'm guilty of overthinking things here."

"Are you blaming your holiday brain now?"

"Not at all. I'm trying to figure out why the killer would choose this location."

"Give it up. I wouldn't bother trying to work that out for now. There aren't that many houses around this area, so whoever killed him would have driven out here. ANPRs, that's got to be a start."

"I agree. We'll get Craig on it, he's a dab hand at working with the cameras. Okay, I've seen enough. Let's head over to see the solicitor."

"Makes sense, we're only wasting time hanging around here. Let Lorraine and her techs analyse the area first, and then we can always come back here and try to work things out for ourselves later on."

THEY ARRIVED at the solicitor's office in the heart of the city around thirty minutes later. Mr Nicholls' secretary said she'd been expecting someone from the police to turn up and showed them through to Nicholls' office.

He gestured for them to take a seat. "Would you like a drink?"

Sara waved her hand. "We'll pass if you don't mind. Thanks for agreeing to see us. Perhaps you can go over the events of this morning with us?"

"Of course. I was out on my morning run. I got to the location at about seven. I usually run for forty-five minutes then go home for a quick shower before coming into work."

"And that's a daily occurrence, is it? At the same location?"

"No, I vary my routes to break up the boredom. I've been running there for a few days. I was shocked to see the man's body swinging from the trees. I saw it from a distance. My eyes aren't so good these days; I wear specs during the day at work but remove them when I'm out for a run. Once I realised what was confronting me, I got out my phone and rang the police immediately. They told me to stay at the scene until an officer arrived. Then the pathologist showed up within fifteen minutes. I asked her if I could leave as I needed to get to work. She said that wasn't a problem and that someone would drop by within a few hours to take my statement. I don't think I've got over the shock yet."

"Sorry you stumbled across the gruesome scene. Did you see anyone else in the area?"

"No one at all. Strange, I usually see a few other joggers down there. Maybe they shied off because of the weather. I'm not as fickle as some folk, out there rain or shine, I am. My fitness means everything to me as my father died young from heart disease."

Sara nodded, completely understanding his need to combat any hereditary illnesses suffered by his parents. "Did you run there yesterday as well?"

"Yes, at the same time."

"And the same route?"

23

"Yes. Ah, I see what you're getting at, you're trying to ascertain how long the body had been there."

Sara offered up a weak smile. "Correct. At the moment, we have very little to go on in the way of clues, so the more questions we ask the better."

"I get that, I truly do, however, I stumbled across the deceased and that's really all I can tell you."

"I don't suppose you recognised him, did you? Maybe as a fellow runner who used the same route as you?"

"No, not at all. Ah, yes, he was wearing sportswear, I see where you're coming from now. That fact never dawned on me at the time. My priority was ringing the police and doing all I could to get the body removed ASAP. You know, sometimes, like on my day off, when I've delayed my run for a few hours, I've seen mothers pushing prams with babies and toddlers down there."

"And we appreciate your thoughtfulness in putting others first at what must have been a distressing time for you."

"Thank you, I try to be considerate where at all possible."

"That's commendable. Is there anything else you can tell us?"

He chewed his lip for a second and shook his head. "Sorry, I think that's about all. I know it's not much in the way of help with your investigation."

"Not at all." Sara rose from her seat.

Carla followed suit.

"I can't thank you enough for reporting the crime to us as soon as you discovered it," Sara said.

"Crime? Are you telling me he didn't commit suicide? It simply never crossed my mind that foul play could be involved. Oh heck, that poor man. Why there? Where families go? Sick, that's what it is, bloody sick."

"I wholeheartedly agree with you. We'll let you get on

with your day now. Thank you again for reporting the incident."

"Of course, I'd say it was my pleasure, except nothing could be further from the truth. I hope it doesn't take you too long to find out who the victim is and that you can track down and punish the evil people who did this to him."

"We hope so, too. Good day, Mr Nicholls."

Sara and Carla left the office, walked back through the reception area and out to the car.

"Where to now?" Carla asked, a sudden gust of wind hitting them square in the face.

"Let's get in the car before the weather turns nasty, which I think is imminent."

They trotted across the car park and jumped in the vehicle.

"What now?" Carla asked. "With no clues to go on, where the heck do we start?"

"We'll go back to the station and work with what we have to hand." Sara planted a friendly punch on Carla's thigh. "Don't be such a defeatist."

"Sorry, all right? Maybe I'm more exhausted than I thought I was."

"Ouch, now I feel doubly bad for taking a break and leaving you to deal with everything at the station."

"Now you're talking utter bullshit. Ignore me, I enjoy wallowing in self-pity. Hey, everyone is entitled to time off. I'll tell you something, guilt won't enter my mind in a few weeks when I jet off to the Balearics." Carla laughed.

Sara started the engine and drew away. "I bet. I'll be sure to remind you of this conversation, though."

"I thought you might."

. . .

"Right, so that's what we have so far, guys. I know it's not much to go on as such, but we've been here before in other cases and breezed through them to arrest the culprits. We're going to need to dig deep, and swiftly, if we're going to catch the perpetrator and bang them up. Craig, I'd like you and Barry to sift through any CCTV and ANPR footage you can gather from the area. I'm not holding out much hope, but see what you can do for me."

"We'll get on it right away, boss," Craig replied.

The two men got to work on Craig's computer.

"Carla, why don't you contact Missing Persons, see what they can come up with?"

"How far back shall I go?"

"If the body was left there yesterday, perhaps go back a week or so. Lorraine said the victim had other bruises. According to the note, he was held somewhere for a few days before the killer finally drove him out to Belmont to do the deed."

Carla nodded. "Gotcha."

"Marissa, depending on what Carla finds out, be ready to give her a hand."

"Yes, boss. Anything I can be doing in the meantime?"

"You can look back over our records, see if there are any other similar cases in the past, where the perpetrator has strung up their victim. Say in a thirty-mile radius, how's that?"

"Nothing's coming to mind, boss, but I'll get digging."

"Good, the rest of you carry on with what you were doing and get ready to jump in and help out if necessary. I'll be in my office, dealing with the dross that has accumulated in my absence."

Sara threw a fleeting glance in Carla's direction; however, her partner chose to ignore the subtle dig and picked up her phone to make a call.

"And a coffee wouldn't go amiss in fifteen minutes or so if someone is up for it."

"Leave it with me," Jill shouted.

Sara winked and gave her a thumbs-up then dipped into her office. She tried to settle down to the paperwork once more but struggled. Her phone rang five minutes later, giving her another excuse to swerve the chore.

"DI Sara Ramsey, how may I help?"

"It's DCI Price. Have you got five minutes, Sara?"

"On my way, you've saved me from a painful half an hour."

"Dreaded 'return to work mundane tasks' eh?" DCI Price laughed. "I'll make sure Mary has a pot of coffee on the go, ready for your arrival."

"Music to my ears. Anything serious, boss?"

"We'll discuss that when you get here. See you in a few minutes."

Sara ended the call and ran a comb through her hair. Then she made her way along the corridor to DCI Price's office, a soupçon of doubt nibbling at her gut as to what to expect from her visit. "Hi, Mary. How's it going?"

"Hey, you're back. How were The Lakes?"

"I am, and what a welcome, eh? It was beautiful up there. We're definitely going to venture up there again soon. Have you ever been?"

"Often. I knew you'd enjoy it. Go in, she's expecting you, and the coffee is dripping through the filter as we speak. It shouldn't be too long."

"I can't wait. A decent cup of coffee is what's needed to see me through the troubled waters."

"That bad?"

"A new case landed on my desk a few hours into going through the dreaded backlog of paperwork. I'm kind of feeling like a duck treading water out in the middle of the ocean right now."

"Bless you, it's bound to get better."

Sara held up her crossed fingers and knocked on the door to DCI Price's office and walked in.

"Ah, there you are. Come in, Sara. Take a seat. You look well rested."

"I was, until I showed up for work this morning."

Carol Price inclined her head. "Oh, what does that mean?"

"It means that we took on another case not long after I sat down to tackle the pile of paperwork gathering dust on my desk."

"Bugger. What type of case?"

"A murder case. Carla reckons the criminals must have heard I was back and crawled out from the woodwork to make my life hell again."

Carol cringed. "The Devil has a knack of knowing these things, doesn't he? Do you know who the victim is?"

"No ID at the scene. He was found hanging from a tree in Belmont Country Park this morning by a jogger."

"Oh heck. No chance it could have been self-inflicted?"

"Not according to the pathologist."

"Well, I'm sure you and your team will soon be able to drill down and get the results needed to arrest the culprit."

"I'm glad you have faith in us. It's going to be difficult with no ID to hand. But you know us, we won't let that stand in our way."

"I'm sure. I've called you in to ask how you felt the team did while you were away."

"The same as usual. Carla coped admirably. All right, they didn't have any tough cases to deal with, and she's already admitted she found the paperwork overwhelming, but it is what it is."

"Ah yes, we can't all be experts like you in that field, can we?"

Sara snorted. "Expert in the art of police paperwork, is there such a thing?"

"If there is, you're definitely it. That's beside the point. Getting back to Carla…"

Frowning, Sara asked, "Is there a problem with her?"

Carol wagged a finger. "No, don't go reading something into this that isn't there."

"Oh, okay, if you say so. Why the sudden interest in what Carla does while I'm on holiday?"

Carol picked up her silver ballpoint pen and studied it. "An opportunity has arisen and…"

"What? Some form of promotion?"

The door opened, instantly halting the conversation between them. Mary delivered the cups of coffee and placed them in front of Sara and Carol.

"Thank you, Mary. We shouldn't be too long. I'm expecting a call from the Super. Will you tell him I'll ring him back in a few minutes?"

"Will do, DCI Price. Can I get you ladies a nice shortbread biscuit to go with your cuppa?"

Sara waved her hand. "Not for me, thanks, Mary. I had a huge breakfast before coming to work. I'll probably skip lunch as well today."

"Really? You have time to cook before leaving home?"

"No, Mark did. He has a full day of operations ahead of him, so it was really out of necessity."

"Bless him. You have a good man there, Sara."

"Lucky lady," Mary agreed with their boss and left the room.

Sara sipped at her coffee, savouring every delicious mouthful as it trickled down her throat. "You were saying?" she prompted.

29

"You know what the Super is like, always on the lookout for bright sparks he can promote. I wondered if we shouldn't put Carla's name forward."

"I think you're asking the wrong person, it's Carla you should be speaking to, not me. While I'm eager for her to put her foot on the promotional ladder, my personal judgement would be that she still has a lot to learn."

"Okay, you know I value your judgement. In which department do you think she's lacking?"

"Putting it bluntly, in every department."

"Well, you've floored me with that response. May I ask why you haven't brought this to my attention before now?"

"Hey, I thought we were talking off the record here. I'm not telling tales on Carla, not by a long shot. All I'm saying is that if you had her in mind for a promotion, I think she should perhaps be tested more. Wait, I still think you should be running this past her, not me, see how she feels about taking a tentative step up the ladder. I get the impression that she's not that interested but, hey, what do I bloody know?"

"I'm asking for your honest opinion. No one knows her better than you do. Are you telling me you don't necessarily believe she's inspector material?"

"Now you're guilty of putting words into my mouth. My point is, she needs extra guidance in certain areas."

"And they would be what?"

Sara struggled to find the appropriate words without dropping Carla in the mire. She paused and chewed the inside of her cheek. "I repeat, I wasn't joking, I'd say all areas."

"What? Umm... wait just a minute here. What you're effectively telling me is that you haven't been fulfilling your duties properly."

Sara's head jutted forward, and her eyes doubled in size. "Christ, if that's what you think..."

THE GAMES PEOPLE PLAY

"Get off your high horse, woman. This is you and me having a friendly discussion about one of your colleagues, nothing official here."

"I'm glad to hear it."

"Nevertheless, you're aware your role also involves bringing on those around you, aren't you?"

"Of course I am, within reason. I thought my main priority was to rid the streets of violent criminals."

"That as well. Blimey, now you have me questioning your role."

"Are you kidding me? I'm not sure that bloody comment is warranted, boss."

"I have no intention of taking it back, Sara."

"That's told me. What are you saying? That you want me to stand down from my role?"

"Don't be so *ridiculous*. No, what you're going to need to do is start conducting monthly appraisals of your team."

Sara closed her eyes and tipped her head back. "Jesus, as if I haven't got enough to do." She opened her eyes again and stared at DCI Price. "Nothing like heaping pressure on someone's shoulders, is there? Undoing all the good a holiday has given them. May I remind you that you're the one who virtually forced me to take the time off in the first place."

Carol held her hands up in front of her. "Cut the attitude. I'd be failing in my duty if I didn't have this conversation with you."

"Why now? Is the Super pressurising you for not bringing people through the ranks?"

"Possibly. Let's not blow this out of all proportion, Sara."

"Oh, okay, silly me."

Carol groaned and threw herself back in her chair. "Now you've fallen out with me."

31

"I haven't. I'm sitting here, wondering where the hell this conversation is going to lead to, and not getting very far."

Carol sat upright once more. "I thought it would be a convenient time to approach the subject, what with you fully refreshed after your holiday and with Carla left holding the fort as they say."

"I feel pressured, if you want to know the truth. I believe this conversation couldn't have come at a worse time. I've had a new case land on my desk this morning and I should be out there, rallying my troops. Instead, I've been called into your office to be reprimanded for not priming my partner ready for a possible promotion, whether she bloody wants it or not."

Carol picked up her pen again and twisted it through her fingers. "Do you want to go out and come back in again?"

Anger mounted and was difficult for Sara to quash. "I'll tell you something, if I walk out of this office in the mood I'm in right now, I won't come back. And that's not a threat, it's a promise."

"Jesus, Sara. I thought we were friends as well as colleagues. Am I not allowed to speak freely and openly now?"

"Not at all." Sara crossed her arms and refrained from saying anything further, not trusting what was likely to drop out of her mouth next.

"Maybe you should get on with your day and we'll discuss the matter later."

Sara finished off the last of her coffee and placed the cup and saucer on the desk. "Maybe that would be a good idea." She stood and walked towards the door. "I'm sorry if during this conversation I said anything that you might misconstrue as offensive."

"You haven't. Wrong place, wrong time. We'll revisit the conversation in the future."

Sara issued the briefest of smiles and left the office, resisting the temptation to slam the door after her. "Thanks for the coffee, Mary, at least that went down well and didn't choke me."

"Excuse me? Am I missing something, Inspector?"

"No, just me being snide, sorry. Back to work for me."

"Have a good day, or should I say, I hope your day improves."

"Thanks, I'll take that."

"Mary!" DCI Price bellowed.

The secretary grabbed her pen and notebook and rapped on the chief's door before she received the all-clear to enter.

Sara left her to it and returned to the incident room. "How's it going?"

Carla was the first to raise her hand. Sara crossed the room to her partner's desk.

"We've got three possible missing persons that I think we should look into."

"That's great news. Get their information, and we'll get on the road. I need to get out of this place."

"Something wrong?"

"I'll tell you later, much later, it's not worth the hassle right now."

Carla gathered her notebook and stood. "I'm ready when you are."

"I'll grab my jacket and join you downstairs. Anyone else got any news yet?"

The rest of the team looked blankly at her and shook their heads.

"Oh well, carry on. The more we dig, the more likely something important will come our way." She dipped into the office to collect her jacket and caught up with Carla in the reception area. "Are you good to go, partner?"

"I am. Are you? What's up?"

Sara pushed open the main door and marched ahead to her vehicle. "Nothing that won't keep. Where are we going first?"

Carla flipped open her notebook, the pages rustling in the breeze. "Over to Rotherwas for the first one."

"Okay, the traffic shouldn't be too bad at this time of day. It can get a bit congested down that way, occasionally."

"You're right. We should get a clear run through around this time. Are you sure you're okay?" Carla asked, concerned.

"Yes, stop worrying about me."

"If you insist, just don't have a go at me for not showing you any sympathy in a few hours from now."

Sara turned and grinned. "I won't. Who are we going to see?"

"Vanessa Chance. Her husband went missing in the middle of last week. She was frantic when I spoke to her earlier. What if it's not him? And he's still missing?"

"Let's knock all the 'what-ifs' on the head for now, it'll only drive us crazy otherwise."

"If you say so."

Carla pointed at the next turning on the right, despite the satnav voice already instructing Sara what road to take.

"Thanks, I'm not deaf."

"Christ, ever since you saw the DCI you've been like a bear with piles."

Sara laughed at the analogy. "I think you've got that wrong but I kind of like your take on it better than the original."

"Which is?"

"A bear with a sore head, not a sore arse."

They exited the car, and Sara glanced over the roof at Carla whose cheeks had coloured up.

"Bugger, I kind of cocked up there," Carla said, "me trying to be a smart arse again, pun intended."

Sara tutted and rolled her eyes to the black clouds over-head. "You're forgiven. We'd better get inside before we get caught in the oncoming downpour."

"You missed your vocation... as a weather girl," Carla grumbled.

They ran towards the semi, big splats of rain hitting them on the back.

"Crap, sometimes I hate being right."

Vanessa must have been watching out for them because the front door opened before Sara had the chance to ring the bell.

"DI Sara Ramsey and DS Carla Jameson, who you spoke with earlier, Mrs Chance."

"Come in out of this foul weather. Pleased to meet you. You'll have to excuse me, I'm feeling a little anxious, have been since I received your call about coming to see me. Please tell me it's good news and that you've found Ian."

"Shall we take a seat somewhere?" Sara asked with a smile.

"Yes, sorry, excuse my manners. Come through to the lounge, or would you prefer to go through to the kitchen? I'm easy either way. Both rooms are tidy. This house has been cleaned ten times over since Ian went missing. I was desperate to keep my thoughts at bay. I guess you'd say my imagination is somewhat overactive."

"I'm sure that's totally normal in the circumstances. Whichever room you prefer."

"The lounge then, let's take a comfy seat. Come through. Can I get you ladies a drink?"

"Not for us, but thanks for the offer."

They followed Vanessa up the short hallway to a large lounge at the rear. The French doors opened out onto a pretty garden laid to lawn with a few borders dotted along the grey-painted fences on either side. The room lacked any

35

kind of knick-knacks or photos, which Sara was hoping to find. The three of them sat, Vanessa on the very edge of her seat, clasping her hands tightly until the whites of her knuckles showed.

"Please, can you tell me what you know? Why you're here? Have you found him? Is he alive? Or have you found a body? That's usually the case when a police officer shows up at your door, isn't it?"

Sara swallowed down the saliva that had seeped into her mouth. "Unfortunately, we were called out to attend a location this morning where a body had been discovered." She raised a hand. "Please, don't get upset. At this stage, we have no way of knowing if the deceased is your husband or not."

"But it's a man's body you found?"

"Yes. Do you have a photo of your husband?" Again, Sara scanned the room in case she had missed one tucked away in a corner somewhere.

"Only on my phone. We're not really the type to have loads of photos dotted around, cluttering up our home. Let me see if I can find it. I had it in the kitchen last, I think. Oh, I don't know, my mind is a mess right now. Well, it's hardly surprising. Ian just up and left me, didn't even pack a bag. I know deep down that something terrible has happened to him. Now that you're here, I'm not sure I want to know what the truth is."

"Let's not get ahead of ourselves here. Why don't you find your phone first, and we'll go from there?"

Vanessa leapt out of her chair and then dropped back into her seat, her left hand holding her cheek. She blinked a few times and inhaled a couple of breaths. "Sorry, I'm not sure what came over me. I haven't been eating well, what with Ian... If you must know, I've been utterly distraught."

"Why don't you tell me where you think you've left it, and I'll fetch it for you?"

"On the worktop, by the sink in the kitchen, I think."

Sara smiled and exited the room. She turned left at the door, presuming the kitchen was the room adjacent to the lounge. She was right. It was beautiful. It seemed to be a new addition to the house, an extension that had taken up half the garden. She shook her head, stopped daydreaming about what a joy it would be to have a sumptuous room like this to walk into every morning, and marched over to the sink which was in the middle of the huge island. She picked up the woman's iPhone and returned to the lounge.

Handing it to Vanessa, she couldn't help herself from gushing, "What a fabulous kitchen you have, is it new?"

"Yes, we only finished it two months ago. Ian did much of the work himself, with help from a couple of friends in the building trade, you know, a plumber, electrician and a plasterer. I pitched in with the decorating, but my contribution was minor compared to the hours of blood, sweat and tears the others put in."

"It's a credit to you. I can imagine how much hard work was involved."

Vanessa nodded. "Thank you. Right, let me try and find a decent photo of Ian." She unlocked her mobile and scrolled through dozens of photos until she found one suitable to show to Sara. "I think this is the best one. I tried to find one that isn't too smiley. He's always playing the fool, never takes life that seriously."

She angled the phone towards Sara and Carla. They both studied it. It didn't take long for Sara to decide that the person she was looking at wasn't the victim found that morning.

Sara coughed to clear her throat. "I'm sorry, it's not him."

"What? Oh God, I don't know whether to feel relieved or disappointed. I'm so confused right now."

"I can understand. Personally, I would feel relieved, and

going forward you can cling to the hope of Ian returning home."

"Maybe you're right. Why did he leave the way he did? If we'd had an argument, I could understand him walking away from me... from our marriage, but we hadn't. We had everything to look forward to." Vanessa gently rubbed her hand over her stomach. "I'm expecting our first child."

"Oh bugger, I'm so sorry. Did Ian know about the baby?"

"No, I only found out at the weekend. My doctor told me to remain calm, as any possible upset could be devastating for the baby."

"I agree." Sara found herself teetering on the edge of a dilemma. She was keen to help the woman but also eager to move on, to try and find the next of kin of the victim who had been discovered in the woods. "I'm sorry, as much as we'd love to help you try and find your husband, our priority must remain with our investigation. What progress have you made with the police, if anything?" Sara couldn't help herself. She hated the thought of this woman being cast aside, especially now that she was pregnant.

"I keep ringing the station every day to see if they have any news for me but I'm often left disappointed. The officer who has been put in charge of my case is very patient with me when I contact him, however, he never has anything new to share."

"Can you give me his name?" Sara withdrew her notebook from her pocket.

"It's Sergeant Renshaw."

"Okay, leave it with me a few days, I'll see what I can do."

Vanessa nodded and offered up a grateful smile. "That would be wonderful, if it's not taking you away from your duties."

"It isn't. You're going to have to bear with me, though."

"Of course, I understand your priorities must lie with the

38

THE GAMES PEOPLE PLAY

investigation," she replied, sadness creeping into her voice. "He'd not long completed the work on the kitchen and was so proud of his achievements. It was the first time he'd taken on a major project as big as this."

"Was anything worrying him? At work or financially? Anything along those lines?"

Vanessa sighed. "I suppose we overstretched ourselves a little. The building costs nearly doubled during the renovations, thanks to Covid. It was a struggle finding the extra funds, and Ian really didn't want to cut corners. He had a vision and saw it through to the end. Why would he walk away after it was completed? That's what keeps going round and round in my head. It doesn't make sense. None of it does."

"And his work?"

"He was, sorry, *is* a chef, a head chef, although he took a few months off to throw himself into the project to complete the renovation."

"And what did his boss have to say about that?"

"He was fine with it, no bother at all. It's quite quiet in the summer anyway, what with us not living in a tourist area."

Sara nodded. "Makes sense. What about his friends? Did you contact them, see if they can fill in any blanks about what concerns he had?"

"Yes, they all said the same. He was thrilled with the work he'd carried out and couldn't wait to start entertaining again. We used to put on frequent themed dinner parties for our friends. There was even talk of Ian starting up a new catering business, but that was going to happen in the near future, once we'd paid off the debts we'd incurred from the build."

"This is my nosey question, and you have every right to tell me to get lost... How much are we talking about to have a state-of-the-art kitchen as beautiful as that?"

"We had planned on it coming in at around fifty grand,

39

but it ended up costing nearly double, around ninety-five, although we still have a few bills to come in for some of the high-end equipment we had on order."

"Blimey, no wonder it's so breathtakingly beautiful. You mentioned your debts. Mind if I ask how much?"

"About forty thousand, but that could increase by around five grand. With the baby on the way, I haven't got a clue how I'm going to pay for it all. I only work part-time at a baker's. Ian is the main breadwinner in the family." She smiled. "That one slipped out, I didn't mean to say that, I promise."

Sara smiled. "I'm so sorry you have this worry hanging over you at this significant time. I hope your family are supporting you."

"They are. Both of our families have been amazing. All the men have been out there every night, searching for him. No luck up until now. It's so frustrating."

"I can imagine. Does Ian have any mental health issues?"

"Not as far as I know. Maybe he disguises it well. He got a bit short with me at one point during the build, once all the bills started rolling in. We had a chat, I worked out all our finances, and he appeared to be okay with it and ploughed on." Her head bowed, and she sighed again. "I just can't imagine what life is going to be like without him. I spend most of the day, when I'm not at work, listening for the front door to open and him calling out that he's home."

"Have you contacted all the hospitals in the area?"

"I rang the main hospital, but not the other ones. Maybe I should do that after you leave."

"Yes, please do. It's possible that he might have had an accident and is suffering from amnesia."

"Oh God, that thought never even crossed my mind. Something drastic has happened, I know that much. He wouldn't have upped and left the way he did, he just wouldn't have."

"Then you need to emphasise that to Sergeant Renshaw—no, I will. Maybe he can sort out a public appeal for your husband's whereabouts, just in case he's out there, suffering from memory loss."

"Sounds feasible to me. I appreciate you wanting to help me out. I feel so lost and inadequate."

"You shouldn't. You need to take care of yourself and your baby. Let's see what we can do to bring Ian home. My apologies, we're going to have to run out on you. We've got two more families to see yet."

"I understand. I hope you find the family you're looking for soon. I don't envy them hearing the news you're going to deliver. That's going to be a terrible ordeal for them." Tears filled her eyes, and she showed them to the front door.

Sara handed Vanessa one of her business cards. "Give me a call if he shows up."

"I will. I can't thank you enough for what you're doing for me on top of your busy schedule. I really do appreciate it."

"It's what we're here for. Keep positive."

"I'll try. Thank you."

Sara and Carla raced back to the car as it was still tipping down and they were both wearing suit jackets as opposed to their winter coats.

"Poor woman. Fancy her feeling that he's run off like that," Carla said. She buckled into her seat.

"If that's the case. Why would he do that if he has everything to live for? Granted, he didn't know about the baby, but even so, there were plans in place to start up a catering business. People who have grand plans don't tend to go missing, do they?"

"Exactly. I'm not personally holding out much hope for

his return. Are you going to have a word with the copper dealing with the case?"

"I said I would. Why would you doubt it?"

"I wasn't. Oh, ignore me, I just thought we've got enough to be going on with, without adding to our workload."

"Not *ours*, mine. I'll see to it. I can't leave her high and dry like that. There must be a simple explanation for him going missing, we just need to find out what it is."

"Good luck with that one. Want me to put the next address into the satnav?"

Sara grinned. "Well, I can't, you're the one with the information to hand, not me."

Carla waggled her head and pulled a face as she input the information.

AFTER A SHORT DRIVE through the countryside, they came to the next house on their list. The home of Jane Turner. The cottage was situated in Holme Lacy, a village Sara had visited a couple of times while she'd been looking to buy a property of her own in the area. Her biggest concern had been how far it was situated from the city although, saying that, the property she had eventually bought had turned out to be the same distance away, but on the other side of the city.

Jane opened the front door; she had spotted them draw up. She'd been expecting them and had been pacing the floor in the lounge. "Hello, do you want to come in?"

Sara could tell the woman was anxious. She showed her ID and introduced herself and Carla. "Thanks for seeing us at short notice, Miss Turner. We're lucky to catch you in, are we?"

"No, I work from home, so I'm here most days. I only venture into the office on a Friday. Enough about me. I gather you possibly have some news about Patrick. Come in out of the rain."

She asked them to join her in the lounge. The ceiling had a huge oak beam running the length of it, and there was a large inglenook fireplace, taking up the entire wall at the far end.

"You have a lovely home, Jane, have you lived here long?"

"About five years. Patrick moved in with me two years ago, and we've slowly been doing up the place. It's a labour of love. This is the first room we tackled. We had to sandblast the beam and treat it for woodworm. Fortunately, everything turned out good in the end."

"You've done well, it's so homely in here. I bet it's really comfy when the fire is roaring."

"Yes, it heats the whole house as well. Just what we need during the cost-of-living crisis. Won't you take a seat?"

Jane settled into the wing-backed armchair close to the fireplace, and Sara and Carla sat on the two-seater Chesterfield sofa on the opposite side of the room.

"First of all, I have to ask if you have a recent photo of Patrick." Again, there were no pictures hanging on the walls or sitting on either of the two windowsills.

Jane picked up her handbag nestled beside her chair and slipped her hand inside. She withdrew her mobile and glanced through her photos until she found one she thought was suitable. "What about this?"

She showed Sara the phone.

Sara shook her head. "No, that's not him."

Tears flowed, and Jane let out a whimper. She dropped her mobile on the carpet and covered her face with her hands. "Thank God. I've been to hell and back." She blew her nose on a tissue she removed from her sleeve and said, "But if it's not him, then where is he?"

Again, Sara knew she shouldn't get involved, but it wasn't

in her nature to ignore the woman's cry for help. "Are you in touch with anyone at the station?"

"Only Karen from the Missing Persons Team. They've been very kind but have told me it will take time to figure out what has happened to Patrick. I don't know what to make of that comment."

"Does Patrick have any enemies?"

"No, not that I know of. No one who would go out of their way to hurt him. I'm sure if he was in danger, he would have confided in me."

"How did he go missing?"

"He went to work last Monday and didn't come home. He always cycled to work. We're trying to be greener in our way of thinking, to cut down on costs."

"What about his phone? Have you tried calling it? It may be an obvious question, but it's surprising how many people forget things like that."

"No, I kept ringing it every day. Now there's nothing, it's just dead."

"What route does he usually take? Where does he work?"

"As an accountant in Hereford. He travels the same route, the one main road into the city, five days a week."

"And have you and your friends searched the area?"

"Yes, every day. A group of us have been out there and found nothing. We don't know where to turn next, in all honesty."

"I'm going to take some notes and see if we've got any spare uniformed officers who can help you out. You said Patrick going AWOL is uncharacteristic for him?"

"Absolutely. I know something bad has happened to him. We were really happy together, talking about our future. Getting engaged and married further down the line was on the cards. I'm gutted beyond words. My life has been on hold for a week. I'm struggling to concentrate on my work. My boss has told me to take time off, but how can I? I couldn't sit here all day, thinking, worrying about what's happened to him, I just can't. I need to have something to distract me, and that's my career."

"What do you do?"

"I'm a designer in the fashion world. I'm freelance, sort of. I work with an agency, hence me talking about having a boss earlier."

"I see. Okay, we're going to have to leave now, however, I want to assure you that I'm going to do my best to assist you. Hopefully, we'll find Patrick or have some news relating to his whereabouts, soon."

"I hope so, I'm going out of my mind here. I'll show you out."

At the front door Sara gave Jane a business card. "Call me if you need me or if Patrick suddenly comes home."

"I will. Thank you."

Once they were in the car, Sara huffed out a sigh. "I feel for both those women. Why should their partners just up and leave like that?"

"What are you saying? That you think there's a connection to our case?"

Sara started the engine. "Fucked if I know. Maybe it's something we should look at once we've tracked down the victim's next of kin. Do you have the next address?"

"Crap, yes, sorry." Carla whipped out her notebook from her pocket and punched the postcode into the satnav.

"I know roughly where that is. We're going to need to head back towards the city centre again."

"We're up and down like a whore's knickers." Carla faced her and grinned.

"Don't tell me, that's gotta be one of Des' gross sayings. I can't see you coming up with something like that, not without thinking about it properly, first."

Carla sniggered. "Actually, it wasn't. I overheard two uniforms having a conversation the other day and caught one of them spouting it, so thought I'd share it at the earliest opportunity."

"There are some conversations that really shouldn't be shared, and that's a prime example."

"Sorry, I didn't mean to cause you any offence."

"Ha, let's be truthful here, no you're not."

"Okay, then, I'm not."

CHAPTER 2

*S*ingleton Way, Tupsley, was a twenty-minute drive away. Sara parked the car outside number fifteen which was a small detached house set back a few feet from the other houses on that side of the road. "Looks as though it's fairly new, as if the house has been built on a spare parcel of land."

"I agree, it's kind of odd and sticks out. Perhaps that was their intention when the architect drew up the design."

Hmm... if it is new, that's three men who have recently undertaken renovation projects on their homes. Is that a coincidence? Or has just about everyone in the entire UK carried out some form of renovation project since lockdown began?

"I said... hey, are you listening to me?" Carla demanded, breaking into her thoughts.

"Sorry, I was miles away. What did you say?"

"That much was bloody obvious. I said I've got a feeling that this could be the end of the line for us."

"End of the line?"

"As in, we could hit the jackpot with this one. I'm hoping so, as we're running out of options now."

"Let's hope so. If not, then we're up the creek as the saying goes. We won't know until we get in there. Are you ready?"

"Yep, willing and able."

"Good, let's go then. I can't see anyone at the window. You did ring ahead, let the wife or girlfriend know we were coming, didn't you?"

"There's a car on the drive, so she must be at home."

"Some detective you are. It could be the husband or boyfriend's car if he chose to go out on foot and never returned."

"I guess we're about to find out what the truth is. She's standing at the front door now."

"What are we waiting for then? Let's get this over and done with." Sara pushed open the car door and got out.

Carla joined her at the base of the incline off the drive and, together, they approached the woman who appeared to be slightly agitated.

"Hello, I'm DI Sara Ramsey, and this is my partner, DS Carla Jameson."

"Pleased to meet you. You'd better come in. I'm Elly Balkind."

"Thanks. Sorry for the delay, we got held up along the way."

"Tractors on the road again?"

"Not this time, although that's the case most days."

Elly led the way through the house, which had an aroma of new paint to it, and into a large lounge-cum-dining room that stretched from one end of the house to the other. Large bi-fold doors at the dining room end showed off a land-scaped garden that Sara felt envious of. She had a reasonably new home herself but had run out of money to finish off the garden. It was a patch of lawn, edged on all sides by wooden fencing. She'd get around to it one day.

Her eye was drawn to a cluster of silver frames sitting on some built-in shelves in an alcove in the lounge area, and her heart immediately sank. *Fuck, it's him. There's no doubt about it.*

"Ah, you're admiring our photos. One of our friends is a keen photographer, and she's always sending us gifts, a new picture in a frame when she's taken a stunning photo."

"She has a good eye. Is that your husband?"

"He's my fiancé. We're due to get married next year, in the spring, if he ever comes back to me. I'm beside myself, there's no reason for Adam to take off the way he has."

"Shall we take a seat?" Sara suggested.

Elly sat on the two-seater fabric sofa while Sara and Carla sat on the cream leather sofa opposite her.

Carla withdrew her notebook and pen, and Sara began the dreaded conversation.

"When did Adam go missing?"

"Saturday. He went to the gym as usual, and I met up with a couple of friends for coffee in the city centre. We usually have a romantic meal on Saturday evenings. Adam is a fabulous cook and is always keen to try out a new recipe he's discovered online. I have no objections to a man taking over my kitchen, I'd be a fool if I did, especially when the results are like eating at a Michelin-rated restaurant."

"I agree. There's nothing better than the man you love taking his turn in the kitchen," Sara chipped in, momentarily speaking from experience as Mark was the main chef in their home. "And you haven't heard from Adam since he left the house?"

"No, which is totally unlike him. He tends to ring me three or four times during the day."

Sara braced herself and sucked in some air. "I'm sorry, Elly, but I believe the body that was discovered in woodland this morning is that of Adam."

"What? Where was he found?" Elly shook her head and placed a hand to her chest.

"Belmont Country Park, do you know it?"

Elly frowned. "Yes, we used to go there quite often, but it's miles away from here, isn't it?"

"That's correct."

"Why? What would he have been doing out there? The last I heard was that he was going to the gym. He went on foot, left his car here."

"Did you check with the gym? See if he showed up for his session?"

"Yes, MuscleBound was the first place I turned to for help. When I got the thumbs-up from them that he'd been there, that's when I decided to call the police and register Adam as a missing person. At first, you guys didn't want to know, told me I could file a report but it wouldn't be actioned for twenty-four hours. I decided to wait and watched the clock tick by throughout Sunday and decided to come down to the station and file the report in person rather than over the phone."

"I'm sorry. The twenty-four-hour rule can be a pain in the rear at times. In our defence, nine times out of ten people tend to crawl out of the woodwork and show up within the time limit. On the odd occasion, such as this, the outcome isn't so positive."

Elly covered her eyes with her hands and sobbed. "Are you sure it's him?"

Sara doubted herself for an instant and glanced at Carla for confirmation. Her partner nodded.

"Yes. I have a photo from the crime scene but I'd rather not show it to you."

Elly wiped her tears on her pretty pink cardigan and picked up a pair of spectacles lying on the coffee table beside her, next to a large ornate lamp. "Can I see it? Please, I need to see him one final time."

"I'm sorry, I don't think you should. You'll get a chance to see Adam after the post-mortem has been performed, which should take place in the next day or two," she said, allowing Lorraine an extra twenty-four hours to carry out the PM, just in case anything else cropped up.

"Oh God, I hate the thought of him being cut open on a stainless-steel table, the blood draining from his body. How did he die?"

Sara considered how well-informed Elly was with the more intricate side of death. "What do you do for a living, Elly?"

"I'm a junior doctor at the hospital. Adam was a vet."

"A vet? Here in the city?" Sara asked. She wondered if Mark would know him.

"That's right, he worked in the practice just up the road. How did he die?" she repeated anxiously.

Sara delayed her response for a couple of moments, hunting for the right words. "A jogger at the location found him hanging from a tree."

Tears flowed down Elly's cheeks. "No, why kill him? Hang on, I'm presuming he didn't do it himself? Can you even tell that at this time?"

"We can. We believe he was murdered. The killer even left a note in Adam's mouth."

"What? What did it say? Was it a fake suicide note?"

"No, the pathologist seems to believe it's a 'method of kill' note."

"A what? Can I ask what it contained?"

"How Adam was going to be killed and how the killer intended to dispose of his body."

"I've never heard of that happening before, is it something new?"

"We've never stumbled across it before, either."

"Oh gosh, I said I would ring them as soon as I knew anything." Elly frantically left her seat and tore out of the room. She returned, punching the keypad of her mobile.

"Who are you calling?"

"Adam's parents. His mother in particular, she'd want to know as soon as possible."

Sara raised a hand. "Please go easy. I wouldn't tell them over the phone. Can you ask them to come over? Do they live very far?"

Elly paused and pressed a button on the phone. "Yes, I never thought about that. I'll ask them to drop round and see me."

"It's a wise decision."

"Hello, Liz, yes, it's me. Is it possible for you and Philip to come to the house? Yes, now, if it's convenient. I have two police officers here with me... we can go over that when you get here... okay, we'll see you soon." Elly jabbed the End Call and threw the mobile on the sofa then flopped down beside it. "That was horrendous. She knows something is wrong, she's not daft."

"Mothers have an instinct when something is amiss. Don't worry, we can handle it when she arrives. I wouldn't have been able to forgive myself if you'd told her over the phone and she had an accident on her way over here."

"I get that. It's a tough predicament. I feel bloody numb, as if an express train has hit me and left me lying on the tracks." She shook her head and ran a hand around her colourless face. "Does it get any better? Knowing that the love of your life has passed away?"

"Speaking from experience, yes it does, given time."

"What are you saying? That you lost someone close to you?"

Sara swallowed and nodded. "My husband. Fortunately

or unfortunately, depending on how you want to look at it, I was there when he passed away."

"Holy crap, you were? Did he die in a car crash or something?"

"No, he was shot. He died in my arms."

"Shot, bugger, how?"

"This isn't about me. All I'm trying to get across to you is that life goes on. I know everyone spouts that at times like this, but it's true. At the time, I never thought I would get over the loss of my husband, but I did. I'm married to a wonderful man now, he's also a vet in the city."

"Really? Who? Maybe I know him."

"Mark Fisher."

She frowned and pondered the name for a moment or two. "Yes, I believe Adam has mentioned him before. I'm glad you found love a second time. I'm not sure I will do the same. Not that I'm on the lookout for anyone else."

"Of course you're not. I didn't mean it to come across like that. Forgive me for being insensitive at such a dreadful time."

"I can tell you didn't mean any harm. I suppose anything said at a time like this is examined carefully, whether it's meant in good faith or not."

"Absolutely. Please accept my apology."

The doorbell rang, and Elly leapt out of her seat. "Christ, they're here."

"Why don't I let them in?" Sara suggested.

"Would you? Thank you."

Sara smiled and left the room. She felt the need to straighten her skirt and jacket on her way to the front door. "Hello, there. I'm Detective Inspector Sara Ramsey. You must be Mr and Mrs Pearce, do come in."

"We are. Where's Elly?" Mrs Pearce asked abruptly, pushing past Sara into the hallway.

Sara pointed at the lounge. "In there."

Once Mr Pearce, who appeared to be the most shell-shocked of the couple, had entered the house, Sara closed the door behind him. She allowed them to go ahead of her.

"What's going on?" Mrs Pearce demanded.

"Please, Liz, take a seat. Here, have mine," Elly insisted.

"I don't want to take a seat. Wait, are those tears on your cheeks? Have you been crying? Have these people upset you, dear?"

Elly faced Sara as if pleading for help. "Mrs Pearce, I'll reveal all once you and your husband are seated," Sara assured the couple.

With a huff, Mrs Pearce threw her handbag on the floor at her feet and flopped onto the sofa, and her husband, who was a smaller man in every way compared to his wife, squeezed on the sofa beside her.

"I'm sorry to be the bearer of sad news, but earlier today, we were called out to a scene. We've confirmed that the body found at the location is that of your son."

Mr Pearce gathered his wife's hand in his own. She shook it off.

"What did you say?" Mrs Pearce snapped.

"You heard, love. Don't make this any harder than it needs to be," Mr Pearce warned.

"My God, in all my days… how dare you speak to me like that, Philip? It was a simple question that I require an answer to." Mrs Pearce turned to face Sara again. "What did you say? I could have sworn you told me that you'd found my son's body. Is that the case?"

Sara's gaze drifted to Mr Pearce who had closed his eyes, obviously reeling from the news. He had no problem understanding what Sara had said. "Yes."

"And you often tell a family that a loved one has departed in a matter-of-fact manner, do you, Inspector?"

"No, not at all. Forgive me if that's the way it came across, that wasn't my intention."

"Well, it did. Elly, how are you, dear? Have they told you how it happened?"

Sara observed Mrs Pearce who was putting on a brave face. Sara knew that the news would hit her hard any second and was prepared for the backlash.

"He was found in the woods, hanging," Elly said quietly.

Sara wondered if the young woman sensed things were about to kick off. As Sara herself was expecting.

"With respect, shouldn't we have been told about our son's death first, his parents being his next of kin? Or am I wrong?"

"That's correct. The reason we initially informed Elly was because we had nothing in the way of ID for your son. We followed up some leads we had. Elly had filed a missing person report. We jumped on that and took a chance. It wasn't until we arrived here and saw the photos of Adam and Elly together that we realised we had come to the right place. This is the third house we've visited this morning in our search to find the deceased's relatives."

"I see," Mrs Pearce said. Her gaze drifted over to Elly. "And you called us right away, I take it?"

"Of course. I could never sit on the news and not tell you, Liz. Please, don't make this situation worse."

"I'm not trying to be awkward. If that's the way I'm portraying myself then I'm sorry. You know how organised I am. I prefer to have all my ducks in a row, and if something comes along and disrupts it, I tend to lash out."

"I know, but surely this needn't be one of those times, Liz. We're all grieving, there's really no need for anyone to fall out, either between ourselves or with the police. We need them to remain on our side. I need to know the truth behind Adam's death, don't you?"

Sara gave an imaginary punch in the air for Elly having the balls to speak out. Liz wasn't coming across as the type of woman you pulled up for making a mistake.

"Okay, I can take a hint. I'll back off. I'm grieving, the same as you are. I happen to have known my son longer than you and feel aggrieved that the inspector here broke the news to you first."

Mr Pearce squeezed his wife's hand and kissed the back of it. "Come now, dear, it's not a competition. What does it matter who was told when? It's not going to bring our son back. We should just accept the situation for what it is and move on."

His wife did her best to remove her hand from his grasp, but he was having none of it and held firm.

"Don't tell me how to behave and what to think, I'm my own person."

Elly groaned and marched out of the room. Sara flew after her and found her standing by the back door, her head resting against the doorframe.

"I can't do anything right in that woman's eyes. I've lost the best person who has ever walked into my life, and here she is... Ugh, I'm shocked, utterly lost for words."

Sara threw an arm around Elly's shoulder. "Don't let her get to you. Some mothers feel overly protective of their sons when a young lady has stolen their hearts. Had you and Adam been together long?"

"Three years. We got engaged two years ago after realising we were soulmates. Up until now, Liz and I have always got on."

"And you will again. She's grieving, you both are. Truth be told, it probably hasn't hit her properly, not yet."

Elly laughed and said, "God help us when it does. I can't go back in there and put up with the mood she's in."

"You don't have to. Let me deal with her. Hopefully, by

the time I get back in there, her husband will have managed to talk some sense into her. This isn't your fault. She needs to realise that, before she can move forward, she must take a step back."

Footsteps echoed behind them. Sara turned to find Liz Pearce standing there, appearing rather sheepish.

"I have an apology to make. You might not want to hear it. I'm sorry for being such a bitch at this tough and excruciating time. I've lost my son, and those are words I never thought would ever leave my lips." She took a tentative step towards Elly who managed to swallow down her anguish and meet Liz halfway.

"It's forgotten. We both want the same thing, Liz, justice for Adam. Pissing off the police won't help our cause."

"That's true. I assure you, I realise that now. Forgive me, Inspector, for speaking out of turn."

Sara smiled. "There's really nothing to forgive. This is an horrendous time for all of you. I want you to know that my team and I will do our utmost to bring the killer to justice, and swiftly."

"Thank you, that's reassuring. Is there anything else we can tell you?" Elly asked, fresh tears cascading down her cheeks.

"Why don't we go back in the lounge and we'll discuss it further?"

The three of them entered the lounge. Sara smiled and nodded at Carla, letting her know everything was in hand once again. They all took a seat. Elly sat on the arm of the small sofa, close to Adam's father.

He patted her hand and smiled up at her. "I'm sorry for what you're going through, what we're all about to go through."

"Thank you, Philip, I'm not sure what to expect now."

"First of all, I want to extend my sincere condolences for

your loss," Sara said. "Secondly, our intention isn't to make things more awkward or upsetting for you, so please accept my apologies in advance if I say anything you may deem insensitive. All we're trying to ascertain is what might have happened to Adam. We can't do that with a blank sheet in our notebooks; that's all we have at present. While I appreciate how upsetting all of this must be for you all, I'm going to ask you to really consider your answers fully, in the hope that we stumble across a nugget of information that will put our investigation on the right track. Again, I must reiterate, at the moment, we have absolutely nothing whatsoever to go on as things stand."

"You have our word that we'll do our very best to work with you and not against you, Inspector, won't we, Liz and Elly," Mr Pearce stated firmly. He reached out and clutched the hands of the two women on either side of him.

"Absolutely. We want to get to the bottom of this mystery, the loss of our son, as much as you do. Ask what you need to ask, Inspector," Liz said.

Sara felt Liz was more at peace with the situation now and had calmed down to a reasonable level, so she went ahead and started questioning them. "In the last few months, has Adam had any cause to raise any concerns about either his work or what was going on in his personal life?"

Philip stared at his wife first and then at Elly. Both ladies shook their heads.

"No nothing is coming to mind," Elly admitted. "I wish we were able to give you the lead you need to begin the investigation."

"I agree with Elly, I can't think of anything," Philip stated. "Adam has always treated those around him fairly and with the utmost consideration." He sighed. "To think otherwise sickens me. What's more, the thought of Adam spending his last hours on this earth at the mercy of someone downright evil, a person who is capable of taking pleasure in ending his life is… well, incomprehensible. It doesn't sit well with me at all. It's going to take a lot to block out such vile thoughts over the coming months or years as we come to terms with our grief. Shocking."

Liz sobbed, and Philip threw an arm around her shoulder and pulled her close.

"I can't believe he's gone, not my baby, our only child."

"I can't either," Elly added. "I know every family probably says this at a time like this, but truly, you have to believe us, in the years I've known Adam, he's genuinely never once fallen out with someone."

"What about at work? Has he had any problems with any of his clients lately? I know Mark, my husband who is also a vet, has a tough time now and again with a pet's owner who has questioned the way Mark has treated his animal."

Elly paused to contemplate her answer before jumping in. "No, I can't think of anything. Maybe it would be better if you asked his colleagues down at the practice."

"What's it called?"

"Pet Care Vets in Eign Hill."

"I know the one. How many vets are there at the practice?"

"Only two. They've been short-staffed for a couple of months now. Ryan, the head vet, has resorted to taking on a couple of trainees to fill the gap for now. They've been under even more pressure this last week, since Adam went missing." Elly plucked a tissue from a box next to her and blew her nose. "I still can't believe it. It's going to be awful referring to Adam in the past tense. That's going to take a while to get used to."

"I know it will. Again, I apologise for putting you through this."

Elly waved her apology away. "You need to ask your questions. Don't worry about me breaking down all the time."

"It's natural for you to get upset. I'd think it very peculiar if you didn't." Sara added a smile to go along with her statement.

"What else do you need from us?" Liz asked, her tone suddenly taut once more.

"Did he have any financial stress?"

Liz frowned. "Nothing. He didn't have any, did he, Elly?"

Elly's gaze dropped to her feet.

"Elly?" Sara prompted. "How long has the house been built?"

"We finished it six months ago, although we're still finding odd bits and pieces to put right here and there."

"And you covered the costs okay during the build?"

"No, costs rocketed because of the pandemic, and we ended up taking out a loan. I told Adam not to, said I would ask my parents for the extra funds needed to complete the work, but he refused. Told me he never took handouts from his parents and he wasn't about to start taking them from mine, either."

"That's right, he was very independent," Philip said. "Although I did offer to lend him some money when I saw he was stressed a few months ago."

"You did?" Liz asked. "Why am I only hearing about this now, from both of you? This family has never had secrets, not regarding something like this. We've always been open with each other. I can't believe both of you have kept me in the dark. Had I known, I would have willingly handed over my savings rather than him take out a loan and pay that off monthly at an exorbitant interest rate."

"It's no good discussing the issue now, Liz, it's far too late," her husband said.

"I know that," Liz snapped. "I'm not stupid."

"I wasn't suggesting you are."

"Please, falling out with each other isn't going to bring Adam back," Elly said, choking back the tears.

The bickering couple fell silent.

"Are you prepared to tell me how much the loan was for?" Sara queried.

"Umm... twenty thousand. It's in both our names, I'm... or I was, paying half of it."

"What? I would have lent it to you," Liz was quick to add.

"It's what he wanted, Liz. Please, the last thing I want to do is fall out with you over something that can't be undone."

"In other words, you want me to keep my nose out of your personal business." Liz crossed her arms and shrank into her seat.

"Stop it, Liz," Philip said. "That's not what Elly was saying, at all. Give the girl a break. We'll talk about this when the officers leave."

"Talking about it now isn't going to solve anything, but you do what you want to do. It's always the same when I speak out about something that irritates you."

Philip glanced at Sara and rolled his eyes.

Sara took the hint and quickly moved on. "Was the loan with a bank?"

Elly nodded. "Oh yes, everything was above board. We wouldn't have used a loan shark if that's what you're implying."

"Again, I'm just trying to figure out if an issue could have led to his death. Is there anything else that you can think of that we should look into at this stage?"

Elly and Mr and Mrs Pearce all stared at each other and shook their heads.

Mrs Pearce was the one who decided to ask a question of her own, next. "When can we see him? You know, to say goodbye."

"I'll pass on your details to the pathologist. She'll be in touch as soon as she's completed the post-mortem. That should take place within the next twenty-four to forty-eight hours."

"I hate the thought of him being cut open. Is that necessary?" Philip asked.

"Unfortunately, it's the nature of the beast when foul play has been suspected," Sara stated, her mouth drying up. She was desperate to leave now; she believed they had covered everything they needed to and was keen to get on with the investigation.

Carla sensed what was going through Sara's mind and closed her notebook.

"We'll be off then, if there's nothing else?"

"There isn't, not that I can think of," Philip replied. "I'll show you to the door, if that's okay with you, Elly?"

"It is. Thank you, Philip."

He eased out of his seat and showed Sara and Carla out. He opened the door and stood back. "Do your best for us, Inspector. Adam meant everything to us. We deserve to know the truth rather than spend the rest of our lives wondering what happened to him and if his death could have been prevented."

"You have my word, Mr Pearce. Once again, we're sorry for your loss. Please, take care of each other. I think Elly is going to need extra support at this time. It might be an idea to call her parents as soon as possible, or perhaps get a friend to come over and sit with her."

"We'll sort that out. She's never alone with us around. We have always treated her like a daughter. That's not about to change now that our son is no longer with us."

"I'm glad to hear it. So many families implode at times such as this, which is a real shame and can be unnecessarily traumatic."

"I can imagine. Will you keep in touch with us, Inspector? Do you have our number?"

Carla flipped open her notebook and jotted down the details he gave her.

"Thanks, hopefully we'll be in touch with some news for you soon," Sara replied. She shook his hand and left the house.

Back in the car, they both exhaled a breath.

"Blimey, I thought things were going to kick off big time back there," Carla said. She buckled up as Sara started the engine.

"You're not alone. So glad Philip was able to calm his wife down before she went for the jugular."

"Is it worth paying the practice a visit, despite what they said?"

"That's the plan. Not everything filters back home, and yes, that's the voice of experience speaking. I know where it is, it's not too far. We'll see what they have to say and then stop off and have a coffee somewhere."

"And some lunch, I'm starving."

"If you want. I'm going to give it a miss today. Mark treated me to the full works this morning, and on top of eating out all last week, I think I've put on ten pounds that I need to figure out how to shift."

"Have you heck. Crikey, you seriously ate out all week?"

"Yep, sometimes a couple of meals a day. Let's just say my hubby has a hearty appetite and leave it there, shall we?"

They laughed.

CHAPTER 3

*S*ara breathed in the aroma of the practice that hit them as soon as they entered. It was a smell she had always found calming for reasons that were beyond her. Two dogs, a poodle and a German Shepherd, were sitting patiently in the reception area, on either side of the room with their female owners.

Sara approached the friendly receptionist and showed her ID. "Is it possible to speak to Ryan? I'm sorry, I don't know his surname. I've been told he's the man in charge around here."

"That's correct. Umm… he's dealing with a patient right now and has two more to see afterwards."

"It's okay, we can wait. Are there any other patients due?"

"No, that's the end of the appointments for the day, although he then turns his attention to surgical matters. He has a couple of dogs that need to be spayed afterwards."

"I can see we've shown up at an exceptionally busy time. Is there anyone else who can help us?"

"It depends. If it's to do with the practice and the way it's run, then I would have to say that Ryan is your man. Other than that, I'd usually suggest you seeing his second-in-command, Adam, however he's not available right now."

"Anyone else, or is it just those two?"

"We have a couple of junior or trainee vets helping out at the moment because we're so busy."

"Would it be better if we came back later?"

Just then, a man in his fifties with a partially balding head appeared in the doorway and said farewell to a woman carrying a cat basket. "Keep her on the tablets for the next few days. If there's no difference then bring her back, Mrs Dickinson."

"Thank you, Mr Smith. Nice seeing you again."

"Take care." He smiled and then spoke to his receptionist. "Right, who do we have next, Helen? Oh, and who are you?"

Sara flashed her ID. "We're the police. We're trying to arrange a time to see you, Mr Smith."

His eyes widened, and he stepped closer to study his diary over the counter. "Not looking likely until later on this afternoon. Is it important?"

"Yes, very. Is there any possibility you can squeeze us in sooner?" Sara crossed her fingers down by her side.

"Give me the diary, Helen, and the surgical one, too." He ran his hand over the pages of both books and groaned. "I have a ten-minute opening at two. I'm willing to forgo my lunch if that will help?"

"That would be perfect. We'll call back and see you then. We don't mind you eating while we interview you." Sara cringed after she remembered what the interview would consist of.

"Very well. Don't be late, I'm a stickler for exceptional time-keeping. Right, I must get on. Lucy, bring Sasha in now, if you would."

"Thank you. We'll see you later," Sara called after him.

He waved. "You will."

"I'll keep the slot free," Helen said.

"Thanks."

"Did you want to see anyone else while you're here?"

"No, we'd better chat with Mr Smith first, but thanks anyway."

"No problem."

They left the practice and stood outside the building.

"Shall we go to Morrisons' café? It's only down the road?"

"If you insist," Carla said unenthusiastically.

Sara peeked at her watch. "It's twelve-thirty. I suppose we could go further afield if you prefer?"

"I don't mind. It's better than what we get at the station, but only just."

"We'll give it a swerve then. Let's see what we stumble across on our drive, how does that sound?"

"A much better alternative, thanks, boss. You always take good care of me."

Sara raised an eyebrow. "I'll remind you of that the next time you accuse me of being hard on you."

They got in the car and drove towards the city centre.

"I know, there's a nice little café tucked down an alleyway, close to Tesco."

"There is? I don't think I know it."

"Mark and I stumbled across it a few months back. Their jacket potatoes are to die for, and the coffee is superb."

"You're ticking all the boxes for me."

Sara parked in Tesco's car park and led the way to the café which turned out to be very busy. "Bummer, I hope we can get a table. Do you mind sitting outside?"

They both studied the clouds overhead.

"I'd rather not, there are some pretty heavy black buggers on the horizon."

"Okay, let me see if I can work my magic on the staff." Sara winked.

"This I have to see."

Sara gave her partner a dig in the ribs. They entered the café. It was buzzing, and there was a slight queue at the counter.

Sara scanned the room and spotted a small table empty in the corner that hadn't been cleared yet. "Quick, over there."

Carla was on it like a shot. Sara remained at the counter, cursing that she hadn't asked Carla what she fancied. She tried to use sign language, but Carla shrugged and pulled a face.

"Do you want a jacket with cheese and beans?"

"I think so," Carla replied, eventually working out what Sara was trying to mouth to her.

"Hi, how can I help?" the young man behind the counter asked.

"Hi, can I get a jacket potato with cheese and beans and a toasted teacake, please?"

"Of course you can. Any drinks for you?"

"Two flat white coffees, thanks. We're on the small table over there?"

"Ah, okay, I'll get someone to come and clear it in a minute. Sorry about the mess, we're super busy today."

"No problem. It's a sign you treat your customers well and the food is good. We're not in a rush, so take your time."

"Thanks for the compliment. That'll be seventeen pounds and fifty pence."

Sara handed him twenty pounds. "Put the rest in the tip jar."

"Thanks, you're too kind. Help yourself to cutlery. I'll make your drinks and bring them over."

Sara smiled and collected the cutlery and a few sachets of sugar from the allotted slots to her right. By the time she reached Carla, the table had been cleared and wiped by one of the waitresses.

"The food looks and smells delicious. Why haven't we been here before?" Carla asked.

"It's one of those places that always slips my mind. You can remind me in the future."

The young man delivered their coffees. "Your food order won't take long. We pride ourselves on prompt service, appreciating the fact that a lot of people visit us during their lunch hour."

"You're always busy, and the food will be worth the wait. I've eaten here before; not as often as I should have."

"Glad you enjoy what we have on offer."

Sara opened a sachet of sugar and tipped it into her coffee and lowered her voice so the customers on the tables around them couldn't overhear their conversation. "I've been reflecting on the cases that have come our way today: three missing men. I know one of them has turned out to be the victim, but taking everything into consideration..." She took a sip from her coffee.

"I'm not sure what you're getting at."

This is one of those instances where Carla falls down on the job, not cottoning on to what could turn out to be vital information. Something to bear in mind when I speak to the chief again. "All three men, or couples should I say, have recently carried out renovations on their properties."

"And you believe there's a significance in that?"

Sara shrugged and took another sip. "It's something that has been playing on my mind. What if there's a connection? We should do some digging, see who the builders of each build were."

Carla thought over the proposition for a moment or two until the waitress delivered their meals. "You're not having a potato? I feel bad now. I'll give you the money for mine."

"Nonsense. I didn't fancy much, just a teacake. Going back to the subject I raised... What do you think?"

"It's a possibility. It's not like we've got anything else we can be tracking right now. Where do you think the other two men are?" Carla blew on her first mouthful of jacket spud and moaned with pleasure once it touched her tongue.

"Good, isn't it? I don't know. I'm going to contact the station, get a few searches organised and see where that leads us. It'll be interesting to see what the vet has to say this afternoon."

Carla swallowed what she was eating and suggested, "Not wishing to step on your toes, but do you think it might be worth giving Mark a call? See if he's heard anything on the grapevine."

Sara pointed at Carla and then tapped her finger on the side of her nose. "See, you're not just a pretty face."

"I have my moments. Bloody hell, Sara, this is delicious, I can't believe we haven't discovered this place before. Although I feel guilty eating alone."

"You're not, I have my teacake. It's yummy, no regrets from me. We'll come here next week, and you can foot the bill, how's that?"

"That's a deal."

Carla continued to tuck in while Sara made a couple of calls. The first was to the station. She spoke to the desk sergeant and explained the situation. He promised to send out a couple of squad cars to trawl the area between Holme Lacy and Hereford to see what they could find. With regards to Ian Chance going missing, that was a different story entirely. But Jeff promised to do his best for her. Then she asked Jeff to put her through to a member of her team.

"Hi, Marissa, it's me. I have a few things I need you guys to do in our absence. Can two of you nip over to the Muscle-Bound Gym? I'm not sure of the address. We know he showed up there, see if anything untoward happened while he was there. Ask if they can supply any CCTV footage as well."

"Okay, anything else, boss?"

"Yes, can you contact the families of the three missing people? Forget that, Adam Pearce is now the name of our victim. The three of them all had recent renovations carried out on their properties. It's been bugging me for a while that there might be a connection. Can you ring the next of kins and ask who carried out the work?"

"Yes, of course. Shall I bring the board up to date while you're out?"

"You're a gem. Thanks. We're grabbing a cuppa before our next interview at two. If you find anything out in the meantime, let me know."

"I'll do that. See you later."

Sara then rang Mark's mobile. "Can you talk?"

"You caught me having a sneaky sandwich in between appointments. What's up?"

"I'm at a café with Carla, the one down the alley near Tesco."

"Don't, that place is amazing. I'm envious of you both."

"I couldn't face anything other than a teacake. She's tucking into a jacket potato, and I think she's struggling."

"They are huge. What can I do for you, Sara? I'll keep eating my soggy tuna sandwich while we talk."

"Sorry, not sorry. I have some bad news for you. I'm going to have to keep my voice down because of the location."

"No, what's that?"

"Do you know Adam Pearce?"

"I do, very well, in fact. Has something happened to him?"

"Yes, sorry, love, he's passed away."

"What? How? He was only young. God, this is a shock."

"I came into work this morning, and Lorraine asked me to attend a murder scene."

"Murdered? Oh fuck! Not Adam. Tell me you've got the person responsible."

"Not yet, but we will. How well did you know him?"

"Quite well. We studied at vet school together."

"I didn't know that, it's not something you ever talk about. Then I'm sorry to have to break the news to you over the phone, love, I really am."

"It's okay. Bugger. How did he die?"

"He was found swinging in the breeze from a tree at Belmont Country Park."

"Bloody hell. You know he was fitness mad, don't you?"

"No, although the last time Elly, his fiancée, saw him he was going to the gym where he works out. Also, he was wearing fitness clothes when his body was found."

"Jesus, I'm having trouble getting my head around this. Why Adam? Was it a chance encounter that ended badly?"

"We don't know, Mark. We've been at it a couple of hours, spoken to his fiancée and parents, but they didn't reveal anything of importance during the interview. You know what it's like, without a lead of any substance to follow up, the investigation could end up being a long, drawn-out one."

"If there's anything I can do to help, you only have to ask, love."

"I know. I was wondering if you'd had any contact with Adam lately."

"Not in months. Last I heard he was building a house in Tupsley. I think that's where he said it was. We used to ring each other regularly up until then. I suppose all his spare time was taken up dealing with the build. It can be stressful organising all the trades, so I've been told."

"I can imagine. The last time you spoke with him, did he sound okay?"

"No, stressed about the build, but then, who wouldn't be? Nothing out of the ordinary going on, if that's what you're asking. Do you believe his death has something to do with his work?"

"We're really not sure, Mark. All we can do is ask the relevant questions in the hope that something comes to someone's mind."

"Let me think about it during the day, and we'll discuss it more when we get home this evening."

"Sounds great. Sorry for spoiling your day, sweetheart."

"Should I give Elly a call, offer my condolences, or would it be better if I left it a day or two?"

"Personally, I would leave it until tomorrow. She was pretty shaken up when we left her."

"God, does Ryan know?"

"We're visiting him at two."

"It's going to rock his bloody world, so be prepared for that."

"Yeah, thanks, Mark. It's never easy hearing that a close friend, business partner, or relative has been murdered. I hope he's able to help us with our enquiries because we've got very little to go on as it is."

"I'll keep my fingers and toes crossed for you. Pass on my condolences to Ryan and tell him I'm here if he ever needs to chat."

"I'll be sure to tell him. Try not to let the news spoil or upset your day. I'll see you later."

"Thanks for letting me know. I'll do my best to block it out until tonight. Love you."

"Ditto, I have keen ears listening."

He laughed, and she ended the call.

"You could have told him you loved him, don't ever worry about me," Carla said. "Your teacake has gone cold now."

"I've gone off it. Here, help yourself, if you're still hungry."

"I'm not. I couldn't eat another thing. Well, maybe a little nibble. Will you cut me some off?"

Sara groaned. "What am I? Your slave? It's not enough that I had to fork out and pay for your lunch already, you'll be asking me to feed it to you next."

Carla placed her hands behind her back and opened her mouth in anticipation. That was until Sara clenched her fist and pulled back her arm, ready to belt her.

"Maybe that was going a bit too far," Carla said.

"You reckon? Eat it. Don't complain if you have problems moving the rest of the day, you hear me?"

"I do and I won't. It's a bit cold but yummy nonetheless."

"Cheeky cow. Want me to ask the waitress to retoast it for you?"

"Is that a word? I think you're having me on with that one, and no, it's fine as it is."

Sara rolled her eyes. "That's a relief."

THEY DREW up in the vet's car park with five minutes to spare.

"Here we go again, all in the line of duty to spoil yet another person's day," Sara said. "The joys and tribulations of being a copper, eh?"

"Or an inspector, at least. I don't envy you, but you're aware of that already. It's not for me."

Sara cringed and thought about the conversation she'd had with Price earlier.

"Are you okay?" Carla asked. "You deserted me for a second there."

"Yeah, I'm fine. Just reflecting on how many lives we've destroyed today."

"Correction, *you've* destroyed."

Sara stepped out of the car and glared at Carla over the roof of her car. "A little support wouldn't go amiss."

"What are you snapping at me for?"

"I didn't mean to, I apologise. I guess I've had enough of ruining people's lives for one day."

"You're forgiven. I'd offer to jump in and fill your shoes for you, except I had enough of doing that last week and could do with the break now that you're back."

"You really do have a way with words today. It's okay, I'll cope, *somehow*."

They walked into the reception area to find Ryan leaning against the doorframe of his room.

"Ah, ladies, glad to see you're nice and prompt. Come through. Can we get you a drink?"

"Not for us, thanks, we've just had one in town."

He closed the door behind them and sat down at his desk.

"Thanks again for seeing us today."

"Take a seat. I'm going to tuck into my lunch, if that's okay with you?"

"Go for it."

Sara shot Carla a nervous glance, and they sat in the two chairs that Ryan had set out for them which seemed out of place in his treatment room. She swallowed and then cleared her throat. Ryan was on his third mouthful of his sandwich before she managed to pluck up the courage to speak. Carla gave her a nudge with her knee.

"This visit is concerning a colleague of yours, Adam Pearce."

"What about him?" he asked, his mouth full of egg mayonnaise and granary bread. "He went missing last week. Apparently, Elly hasn't seen hide nor hair of him. I'm appalled if you must know, but I wouldn't tell her that. We had a full diary last week, and I was forced to take on extra staff which wasn't easy. That added time to my workload I didn't have to spare. I'll tell you something, he'd better show up soon or I'll be forced to replace him. I've got a holiday booked at the end of this month, and there's no way I'm going to miss out on a sunny trip to Mexico, given the dreadful weather we've been having this past month. My family have been looking forward to it all year."

"We're aware that Adam went missing. In fact, our previous appointment was with Elly and his parents."

"Oh, I see. May I ask why, or are you going to tell me to keep my nose out? Has he done something illegal while he's been away, is that it? And you had to break the news that he's been arrested?" He tore at his sandwich once more.

"No, nothing could be further from the truth. It's with regret that we're here to inform you that Adam's body was found this morning."

He stared at her, his mouth gaping open, his chewed-up sandwich on view until he slammed it shut again and swallowed his food. "My God, this can't be true. He's dead? How? No, I can't believe this. I've spent the last damn week bad-mouthing the poor sod, and all the time he was... dead." He threw the rest of his sandwich in the bin beside him.

"Sadly, yes, but we believe he was killed yesterday or during the night."

"Does that mean someone was holding him somewhere before they killed him? Does that sort of thing truly happen? I thought it only existed in novels or films."

"More often than I care to mention. What I'd like to know is if Adam has had a run-in with either another member of staff or a customer in the last month or so."

"Christ, let me think about that for an instant... er, categorically not. Adam was the nicest person I've ever had the pleasure of working with. I'm a grouchy bastard at the best of times, the staff will tell you. He was the yin to my yang, we complemented each other wonderfully. Nothing was ever too much trouble for him. He worked late, when I pleaded with him to, if an emergency operation had to be scheduled. He always took over my surgeries if one of my daughters had a drama of one sort or another, which happens all too frequently. Damn, I'm going to miss his smiling face around here. I'm riddled with guilt now for cursing and calling him every known name in the bloody universe, and all the time he's been treated abysmally which ultimately led to his death. Christ, how have Elly and his parents taken the news?" He raised a hand. "That was a particularly stupid question, please ignore it."

Sara smiled. "Nevertheless, an obvious one. They're all devastated, but at the same time they're eager to learn the reason behind his kidnapping and murder."

"I bet. Jesus, I'd be pacing the floor for days, chomping at the bit to get my hands on the bastard if someone did that to one of my kids."

"I agree. Can you tell me if Adam was worried about anything in the days before he went missing?"

He contemplated the question for a few moments and then shook his head. "No, nothing that he ran past me. We've got a very busy practice here. That means we tend to put our heads down and crack on with things, no time for sharing pleasantries as such. Once a month, time permitting, we caught up with each other to discuss cases, but that wasn't about to happen until next week."

"What about other members of staff? Is there anyone close to Adam? A practice nurse perhaps? Someone who assists him with his patients?"

"Speaking to Dana would be best. I can see if she's available if that will help?"

"It would, thanks."

He dashed out of the room and returned with a young, dark-haired, slim nurse. "This is Dana. I'm sorry if this comes across as insensitive in the circumstances, but my next appointment is here for their surgery, and the owner is keen to get away. He's a taxi driver and has a job to go to."

"That's fine. Thank you for seeing us at such short notice. Can we speak with Dana somewhere else?"

"In the break room should be okay. All the lunches will be over and done with now. Good luck with your... umm... investigation, Inspector."

"Thank you."

"If you'd like to come this way." Dana led them through a winding narrow hallway to a room at the rear that had metal bars at the window.

Sara wasn't surprised about that, given the amount of drugs on the premises.

"What's this about?" Dana sighed and leaned against the sink unit.

"Do you want to take a seat? I think you should," Sara suggested.

The three of them sat at the table that was filled with crumbs, the remains of lunch the staff hadn't bothered to clean up.

Dana leaned back and again crossed her arms. "So? Have I done something wrong?"

"No, this isn't about you at all. Ryan hinted that you might be able to help us with our enquiries."

"Into what? I've never had to deal with the police before. Forgive me if I'm coming across as a tad uncomfortable in your presence, it's because I am."

"There's really no reason for you to worry." Sara inhaled and exhaled a couple of short breaths. "Our enquiries are concerning a colleague of yours, Adam Pearce."

Her hand slapped against her chest. "Oh my, has he been found? Did he have an accident? Has he been in hospital all this time? I had a feeling something bad had happened to him, but what, I had no idea."

The questions came rapidly, and Sara didn't have the heart to interrupt the young woman mid-flow. "Sadly,

Adam's body was discovered earlier today. We're treating his death as murder."

"What? Oh fuck. I can't believe what I'm hearing. Not Adam, he can't be dead, he just can't be. He had everything to live for. He was so excited about the wedding. Marrying Elly. God, I bet she's bloody mortified. She does know, doesn't she?"

"Yes, and his parents have been told as well. I'm sorry if this has come as a shock to you. Obviously, we're going to need to ask you some questions. Are you feeling up to it?"

"Me? I hope you're not insinuating I had something to do with his death."

Sara frowned and shook her head. "Not in the slightest. What we're trying to ascertain is whether Adam had any causes of concern at work in the weeks leading up to his disappearance."

"Gosh, let me think. Hang on a second, yes. He had a mini confrontation with one of the customers."

"He did? Care to enlighten us?"

"Can I take a moment to sort my mind out first? Better still, I could get the relevant file."

"Thanks, that would be extremely helpful."

She raced out of the room and returned before Sara and Carla had a chance to share their views on what they'd learned so far during their visit.

Dana placed the file on the table and dropped into her chair. She ran a finger over the details. "This guy came in a week before Adam went missing. We had our backs against the wall, but he stormed in here at a quarter to six on the Friday evening. Adam didn't have it in his heart to turn away any animal that was suffering. The poor Staffy was breathing heavily, struggling, she was. So Adam took her in, offered to keep her overnight. I actually volunteered to stay with her during the night as Adam had plans with Elly that evening.

78

He put the pup on a drip and popped back at six in the morning to see if there was any improvement in the dog. There wasn't. He rang the owner, asked if the dog might have swallowed something she shouldn't have. The owner couldn't tell him. Therefore, Adam did an x-ray and then performed an emergency operation. I stuck around to help out. I was shattered but at least I'd managed to grab a couple of hours' sleep during the night."

"And what did Adam find when he opened the dog up?" Sara asked, intrigued.

"A whole mass of things. Rags, a torn-up tennis ball, fresh bones from the butcher's." Dana fell quiet.

"Are you okay? Can you tell us what happened next?"

Tears formed and trickled onto her cheeks. "The poor dog's heart gave out under the anaesthetic. Adam tried and tried to resuscitate her, but the dog was too exhausted to respond. She slipped away."

"Oh no, how awful. I bet the owner kicked off, did he?"

"Yes, Adam struggled to contact him all day because he was on the road. The guy finally rang the practice at five-thirty that evening. I'd gone home by then, dead on my feet, I was. Umm… the next day, Adam rang me, said the owner had pinned him up against the wall and threatened to bash his brains in for allowing his dog to die when there was nothing wrong with her. Christ, really? The dog must have been in agony. Stupid bloody moron. If he'd kept a closer eye on what the dog was eating, maybe Adam could have saved her."

"Exactly. What happened next?"

"Adam told me that he'd pleaded his case with the bloke and promised that he would cancel the payment for the operation, which would have run into the thousands. That's the type of vet Adam was. You'll never meet a more caring one, I swear you won't."

79

Sara smiled. "My husband is very much from the same mould as Adam. They were friends and went to vet school with each other."

"Oh, I'm sorry, I didn't know. Does he work in Hereford?"

"Yes, he's Mark Fisher."

"I know Mark. Wow, and you're his wife? I didn't know you were a police officer. I've heard him mention you a couple of times when Adam and Mark have had a conversation over the phone, when it's been on speaker."

"Mark is very upset by the news and sends everyone his condolences."

"I'll be sure to pass them on. He doesn't want a job, does he? We're going to be snowed under for the foreseeable and could do with someone of his expertise."

"I'll ask but I think he's pretty settled running his own practice and all that entails. Would it be possible to have your customer's address? I think we need to have a chat with him before the day is out."

"Of course."

Dana spun the file around, and Carla jotted down the information.

Dana sniffled. "I find it incredibly hard to believe, if this man hurt or killed Adam, that it was because of an animal… one that Adam did his darndest to save, we both did. Oh God, you don't suppose he could come after me next, do you?"

Sara shook her head. "Let's not get carried away here. All we're saying is that he's a likely person of interest, not that he's the perpetrator, so I really don't feel you should be worried at this stage."

"I hope you're right. I'm too young to die, I'm not even twenty-five yet. At least Adam had a few years of life to enjoy before he was taken from us. Oh shit, I can't believe I said that out loud."

"It's fine. We're not going to hold it against you. Is there anyone else you can think of who has recently caused problems or fallen out with Adam?"

"No, only this bloke, Mick Graves. He's a bruiser, so be warned. A hefty bloke. Maybe you should consider taking a male copper with you in case he kicks off."

"Thanks, we'll take your advice on board." Sara stood and tucked her chair under the table. "We'll leave you to it."

"I hope you find the answers you're seeking. Do you think it would be all right if I rang Elly, tell her how sorry I am?"

"I'd leave it a day or two. She'll be going through the grieving process, and who knows how hard that's going to hit her?"

"Oh yes, you're right. Maybe I'll drop her a card and tell her I'm thinking of her instead."

"That might be a better idea. Thanks for speaking with us. Sorry to be the bearer of such bad news."

"Can I tell the rest of the staff?"

"I'd run that past Ryan first. He might prefer to be the one to share such news with your colleagues."

"Gosh, what must you think of me?"

"Nonsense, I see a young woman, devastated by her friend's death."

"I am. Thank you for being so understanding."

SARA FINALLY SUCCUMBED and took Dana's advice and arranged with the desk sergeant to have a patrol car attend the address with them.

Mick Graves' lorry was parked up outside the terraced house when they drew up. Sara had a brief chat with the uniformed officers, telling them what was expected of them before the four of them approached the house. She rang the bell and removed her warrant card from her jacket pocket.

81

The rain had appeared again and was drowning them while the man took his time to answer the door.

Inching it open, he stuck his head through the narrow gap. "Yeah, what do you lot want?"

"Mr Graves, I'm DI Sara Ramsey. We'd like a brief chat with you if you don't mind?"

"I do. I've only this second got in. What's all this about? If someone has said anything about me, it's all lies and they're causing grief that I can do without."

Not liking his tone, Sara said, "I think it would be better if we conducted this interview down at the station."

The door swung open to show Graves wearing a white vest that had a selection of stains down the front. "What? Interview for what?"

"If you'll come willingly with us, sir, it'll make things a lot easier. If not, we can take you in for questioning in handcuffs, if that's what you really want. The choice is yours."

"I'm not shifting from this frigging spot until you tell me what this is all about. I know my rights."

"I'm sure you do. Okay, we need to discuss a confrontation you had recently at the local vet's, with Adam Pearce."

"I know him. He's the one who allowed my dog to die. Yes, I had a few choice words I needed to say to him. Don't tell me he's made a complaint now, after all this time?" He let out a full belly laugh.

"For your information, sir, Adam was killed."

His laughter came to an abrupt halt. "What the actual fuck? And that's why you're here in force, banging on my door, to arrest me for his murder? You need your fucking heads read. I ain't having this. You're not dragging me down no cop shop and pinning this one on me. No bloody way."

"All we're trying to do is get to the bottom of an argument you had with Adam. Come with us willingly, and it will go in your favour. Should you refuse, then it's only going to make matters much worse."

"Worse? Could it get any worse? You're here to frame me for something I ain't done. I'm on the sodding road most days. I ain't seen that twat since he killed my dog. That's all I've got to say about the issue. So fuck off."

He attempted to slam the door shut, but the two uniformed officers shoulder-charged it and sent him reeling backwards.

"Oi, you can't come in 'ere like this. Accusing me of something I ain't done. I'll see what my solicitor has to say about this."

"That might be a good idea, to have them at the station with you during the interview."

"Interview for what? I'm telling you, I ain't done nothing wrong. You have to believe me."

"Cuff him and take him back to the station," Sara ordered.

No matter how much Graves objected, Sara was adamant she wanted to conduct the interview in the safe environment of the station. The uniformed officers marched him out of the house and placed him in the back of their patrol car.

"Do you have your keys before I secure your house?" Sara called after Graves.

"No. They're on the sideboard in the hallway."

She dipped her head around the door and was instantly hit by the stench emanating from the kitchen. *I have no intention of investigating what that bloody is. It's rancid!* Covering her nose and mouth with her cupped hand, she removed the keys from a small china bowl and secured the front door then joined her partner back at the car.

"I didn't venture too far in there, the lingering smell made me retch."

"Yuck, why am I not surprised, given the state of his vest?

Is it any wonder his dog died? She ate just about anything she could get her paws on by the sounds of it."

"Sadly, maybe we should bang him up for animal abuse. Perhaps he took it to the vet's knowing it had eaten all that crap, with no intention of ever paying the bill."

"You could be onto something there, he looks the type. Fucker, making the poor animal suffer like that."

"Right, I need you to contact the team, let them know what's going on and ask them to do some digging on Mick Graves, see what surfaces."

"Are we going to take bets on this one?"

Sara smiled. "Nope, I think it's a foregone conclusion."

AND IT WAS. It turned out that Graves had an Actual Bodily Harm charge on his record that went back ten years.

"Thanks, Christine. It's better to be forewarned. I'm just waiting for the nod from Jeff. His solicitor is due, then we can get down there and tackle him. In the meantime, have you guys got anything for us? What about the gym?"

"Marissa and Barry went to the location and returned with the footage. They're going over it now," Christine replied.

Sara moved around the room. "Anything, guys?"

Marissa paused the footage and opened another tab on her screen. "We've got Adam Pearce leaving the facilities here, at just after six-thirty. It was a pretty vile night, raining."

Sara peered over Marissa's shoulder. "Nothing new there. Was he followed? Any suspicious cars or vans hanging about?"

"Nothing so far, although in fairness, we've only just started going through the footage."

"I know I'm expecting a lot. It's the thought of having to

deal with other victims, that's the driving force behind my urgency to find the perpetrator on this one, taking into consideration what was found on the note with the first victim."

"I understand, boss. Leave it with us."

The phone rang. Christine answered it and gave Sara the thumbs-up that the solicitor had arrived.

"Time to get cracking on this scumbag. Sorry, that was grossly unfair of me calling him that."

"Was it? I'd say you've called it right. It'll be interesting to hear what he has to say for himself."

As it happened, Graves said quite a lot. Sara was aghast that he hadn't gone down the 'no comment' route. She suspected there was a reason for that, because as much as she detested admitting it, he was probably innocent. He insisted that he hadn't seen or gone near either the victim or the gym the night Adam had gone missing and he had what he called 'cast-iron alibis' to prove it. While Sara continued grilling the suspect during the tense interview, Carla left the room to chase up the man's alibis. Sara's partner invited her to join her outside the interview room around thirty minutes later.

"Anything?" Sara asked.

"Nope, everything checks out. There was no hesitation from either party, and there's no way he could have got to them after we brought him in: he hasn't had access to his phone."

Sara took on 'The Thinker' pose and said, "Umm... but there's a possibility that he could have prewarned his mates, got them to make up an imaginary meet-up to cover his tracks in the likelihood of the police knocking on his door in the future."

Carla cocked an eyebrow and folded her arms. "You really

think he's capable of organising that? I don't. As much as I hate to say it, boss, I think we're reading something into it that clearly isn't there. He's a mouthy, arrogant pig, there's no denying that, with an ABH charge to his name, but as far as being a killer, I have my doubts."

"May I remind you that his dog died. If someone had been responsible for Misty's death, I think I'd be livid and go all out for revenge."

Shock etched into every crevice of Carla's face. "Really? Are you sure about that? Isn't that how you and Mark met in the first place? Because someone had poisoned Misty and you needed to seek advice from a local vet?"

Sara cast her mind back and couldn't help but smile. "Sorry, that's inappropriate, me smiling. It's where that emergency situation led to that is tickling my fancy."

"And a whole lot more over the years since then, I shouldn't wonder." Carla chuckled.

"All right. This isn't about me. What are we going to do about him in there? Do we let him go?"

"I would. It's not like we've got anything else on him. He's on the road most days, travelling the length and breadth of the country, from John O'Groats to Land's End; his boss confirmed his extensive schedule. He told me he's never missed a day's work and was super reliable."

"I suppose if he had gone after Adam, the opportunity would have arisen for Graves to have ditched his body further afield."

"You've hit the nail on the head. We're going to have to set the miserable bastard free, our hands are tied."

"As much as it grieves me to say it, I think you're right. Er... that came out wrong, I wasn't saying that..."

Carla rolled her eyes. "Stop bloody digging. Quit while you're ahead."

"Okay, if you insist. Right, I'm going to go in there and

tell him he's free to go, but I'm still going to keep him at the top of our suspect list."

Carla shrugged. "Listening to that gut of yours again?"

"It's all I've got at the moment. We'll set him free then wind things up for the day. Welcome back, Sara!"

"Go on, admit it, it's like you've never been away."

"I hate it when you're right."

CHAPTER 4

The investigation was in full swing, and over the next few days, Sara was pleased that everything appeared to be slotting into place, although she suspected a few major parts of the puzzle were proving to be elusive. She glanced at the whiteboard, and her gaze drifted back to Mick Graves' name several times. However, the more they dug from different angles on the guy, the more her irritation mounted. They'd found absolutely nothing.

"I can sense the frustration growing." Carla offered her a mug of coffee and stood beside her.

"Okay, Einstein, you tell me what we're missing here?"

"The honest answer to that is, I don't know. This case is beyond me. Nothing major has come to light, I'm aware of that as much as you are. Do you want to go over the clues or evidence that is kicking our butt so far?"

Sara groaned. "Let's be fair, that would take us all of ten minutes, so would it be worth it?"

It wasn't until mid-afternoon that their long, drawn-out day got far worse. Sara received another unexpected call from Lorraine, requesting her attendance at Breinton. En route to the location, Sara's stomach tied itself into large Celtic-type knots.

"Bugger, why here? I love this place. Why do frigging killers persist in using this beauty spot as a kill zone?"

"All right, calm down. You know the reason for that as well as I do. It's easily accessible by road but also far enough off the beaten track for someone to risk dumping a body here. Wait, didn't you say the woman's body was found in the river?"

"That's what Lorraine told me, the *only* thing she told me. Why?"

"Well, at this time of year, and especially with all the rain we've had this past week, I'm guessing the river is fast flowing, therefore, the body could have travelled a fair distance. It might not have emanated from here."

Sara winked and tapped her nose. "I like your logic. See, you surprise the hell out of both of us when you put your mind to it."

"Bollocks. Logical thinking has always been a forte of mine, given the chance."

"What are you saying? I suppress your eagerness to offer any suggestions during an investigation? I assure you, nothing could be further from the truth. While we're on the subject…"

"What subject? Have I missed something?"

Sara ignored Carla's last comment and repeated, "While we're on the subject, the boss told me the other day that she's introducing monthly appraisals for the team."

Frowning, Carla faced her and leaned forward slightly. "Appraisals for what? Is she unhappy with our work?"

Sara brought the car to a halt alongside a couple of SOCO vans and one belonging to Lorraine. Other than that, the area was empty. Crime scene tape had been strung across the path around a couple of trees, preventing walkers approaching the pathway that led down to the river.

"No, it's simply something she wants to introduce. I think she's had the Super breathing down her neck and needs to be seen doing something active."

"That's bullshit. How do you feel about the extra work that's going to entail for you?"

"I'm absolutely thrilled... not! Jumping for joy, or I would be, if we weren't about to investigate yet another crime scene."

Carla laughed. "I had a feeling that would be your response. Christ, yet more paperwork for you to drown in. What the heck is the Force coming to these days?"

"I think we should leave that debate until we have a spare full twenty-four hours to discuss it, not the five minutes it's going to take us to get down the hill to the river. You up for this?"

Carla held out her hand. "It's spitting, there's a surprise. What about suits? Should we put one on? They'll probably be sodden by the time we get down there."

"We'll take them with us. I've got a carrier bag in the boot."

Once Sara had collected the required protective clothing, they set off. "Shit, it's muddy as hell down here. I never knew how dangerous this hill could be in the wet."

"Not something we usually encounter. I don't anyway. I'm only ever down this way on a beautiful summer's day."

"Hark at you. It is a stunning location. Shame the dregs of society set out to spoil that image for others."

They marched through the wooded area and stumbled across Lorraine at the edge of the River Wye which, as Carla had suggested earlier, was flowing much faster than normal.

"Hey, Lorraine," Sara shouted from ten feet away. "Is it worth us slipping on a suit?"

"Always worth it. Come over and join the soggy suit brigade."

"Great. You heard her, let's get cracking."

They stepped into their suits and covered their shoes and boots with the blue slip-ons, then approached Lorraine who was examining the victim.

"What have we got?" Sara asked. "And please, don't tell me it's a dead body."

Lorraine glanced up and grinned. "Would I? All right, a walker said his dog was barking at something caught on the riverbank. He plunged down the muddy incline after he realised it was a woman, so yes, the crime scene has been trampled over, and I'm not happy about it."

"Give the bloke a break, he thought he was doing the right thing."

"In this instance, I don't think it matters, but I do wish the general public would take a moment to think and hold back now and again. Really thought about what damage their heroic actions might cause. It's not rocket science, is it? It's a bloody crime scene, for fuck's sake."

"All right. Calm down, Lorraine. These things happen. Speaking personally, if I saw someone in dire need of help, lying facedown in the river, I think I'd jump in first and ask questions later. I'm sure you'd do the same if it came to the crunch."

"I doubt it. You got one thing right, she was facedown. That would be the clue I would need to know to stand well back."

Sara wagged her finger. "You're a harsh woman, Lorraine Dixon."

"It's been said many a time over the years. I go to bed and can sleep at night. My conscience clear because I always say what's on my mind."

"Going back to the victim... Was there any ID found on, or near, the body?"

Lorraine pointed at a plastic evidence bag lying on the grass. Sara approached it. A woman's purse was inside.

"Can I take a peep?" Sara snapped on a pair of blue nitrile gloves and picked up the bag.

"Now you're properly equipped, go right ahead."

Sara grinned and slotted her hand into the plastic bag and removed the purse. She flicked open the catch to see if there was any form of ID inside. There was, the woman's driving licence. "Bingo, that makes a change." She approached the female's corpse and compared her to the photo ID. "There's no mistaking it's her, even with the extra smile in her throat. She lives on the other side of town. No sign of a dog running around?"

"There was no other dog in sight, apart from the one over there with the witness who is sheltering under the clump of trees. I told him you wouldn't be long. He's retired, said he wasn't up to much today, so he was willing to hang around and wait for you."

"Thanks, we'll have a brief chat with him. Good job he's wearing waterproofs if he dived in and pulled the body out."

"Dived in? Hardly, he slid down and dragged her up onto the bank. Weren't you listening to me?"

Sara pulled a face at the pathologist. "I'll be back shortly."

Carla joined her, and they approached the dog walker who was in his sixties, possibly seventies.

"Hello, sir. I'm DI Sara Ramsey, and this is my partner, DS Carla Jameson. Thank you for what you've done here today, I appreciate how upsetting this must have all been for you."

"It was. I'm Ted Jones. I couldn't leave her lying there in the mud like that. I've got a daughter her age. It was Rufus here, who found her. He can be a pain in the rear at times, barking at lumps of wood or large stones he discovers on the riverbank, but this time, there was something different about his bark that drew my attention. I apologise for moving the body, I now realise it was the wrong thing to do. I was keen to assist the poor young woman. I should have known it was too late, but we do what we can in such instances, don't we?"

"Don't worry, as far as I'm concerned you did the right thing. Ignore my grouchy pathologist friend. She means well; she's all for preserving a crime scene. Her job is on the line if there are too many slip-ups."

"Oh damn, I never even thought about someone getting into trouble. How can I make amends?"

"You can't. All you can do is tell us if you saw anyone in the vicinity when you came down here. Or perhaps spotted a loose dog roaming the area?"

"Nothing like that, I'm afraid. I would have tried to capture the dog. They often have a contact number on their collar, don't they?"

"More often than not. Don't worry. Are you sure you didn't see anyone else in the area?"

He shook his head. "No one at all. I parked up the hill, and there was no one else around up there either."

"Okay, we're going to need your address, sir. I'll send a uniformed officer around within the next twenty-four hours to get a statement from you."

"That's fine. Not that I can add anything else. Can I go now? Only Rufus is getting a little anxious. He's not one for being on the lead all the time, and I thought it best not to let him off because he'll only get under the professionals' feet, hampering their progress."

"Yes, you're free to leave. The station will be in touch soon."

He gave them his address and phone number, which Carla scribbled in her notebook, and went on his way. Once he had passed the techs, he let Rufus off his lead, and the cocker spaniel bolted up the hill towards the car park.

"Nice man. Shame his day has been spoilt. Let's see if Lorraine has got anything else to tell us before we get on the road again," Sara said.

They returned to the crime scene.

"What about the woman's mobile?" Carla asked.

"There was nothing in the evidence pile. I'll ask." But first Sara scanned the bags again in case she'd initially missed the phone. She hadn't. "Lorraine, am I pushing my luck asking if you've found her mobile?"

"Yes, you're definitely doing that. If it's around here, we haven't stumbled across it yet. However, look around you, at how tall the reeds are in the water, and it would seem the grass hasn't been cut for a while either."

"I had noticed. It's probably full of bloody tics, too."

Lorraine winced and rubbed her arm. "Lucky we're wearing white. I hear that's supposed to deter them."

"Really? I've not heard that before. Anything else for us before we go and ruin yet another person's bloody day?"

"Nothing so far. Although I have spotted a few restraint marks around her wrists and ankles. Only slight ones, but they're still there all the same."

"Okay, so she was held captive, is that what you're suggesting, in a roundabout way?"

"Possibly. Again, I'll know more once I get her on the table and cut her open. Let's hope she's a good talker."

Sara gasped and poked her friend's shoulder. "Lorraine, that's awful."

"What? It's the truth. It's surprising how many of my patients open up to me once they have nowhere else to go and before I plunge the scalpel in."

"Umm... I think I've heard enough. Keep talking like that and Carla's lunch is going to resurface."

"Hey, don't bring me into it, it's not bothering me."

Sara shot her partner a warning glance, and Carla had the grace to turn away.

Lorraine laughed. "I love it when you get irate. You're such an easy person to wind up."

"Bollocks, Lorraine. If there's nothing else then we'll hit the road."

"I think that's a grand idea. It's early enough in the day, so I'll be sure to get the PM report over to you by this evening."

Sara started to walk away but stopped mid-step. "If you would. Just out of interest, have you looked inside her mouth?"

Lorraine stared up at her and inclined her head. "You're thinking there's a possible link to the Pearce case?"

"I'm not sure. I thought I'd throw it into the mix, just in case."

Lorraine inched open the victim's mouth and closed it again. "Nothing there."

Sara breathed out a relieved sigh. "Okay, well, that's one thing, I suppose."

"Umm... I wouldn't dismiss the idea out of hand," Carla chipped in.

"Why not?" Sara asked.

"It depends how she ended up in the river. Presumably the killer disposed of her body after the deed was done if her throat was cut. Maybe he didn't finish the job off properly and she was still alive when she was dumped in the water and the note was left in her mouth, perhaps it slipped out when she cried out for help."

Lorraine nodded. "Carla might have a point. Maybe we'll keep the idea in mind for now."

"What we're effectively saying, and I hate to say this out loud, is that until we catch the bastard or bastards kidnapping and killing people in Hereford, we're going to continue to link the crimes."

Lorraine shrugged. "Possibly. What's the alternative? To ignore them?"

Sara thumped her clenched fist against her thigh and winced. "Ouch, that was harder than I intended. Okay, we'll go now. Be in touch soon, Lorraine, sooner if you discover anything important you think I should know."

"You have my word. She's safe with us."

On the way back to the car, Sara rang the station and spoke to the Missing Persons Team who confirmed that Bonnie Rogers had been reported missing the day before by her mother, Lisa Rogers.

THE DETACHED HOUSE was much grander than Sara was expecting. "Nice place. Her parents must be quite well off."

"Is it the same address on her driving licence?"

Sara checked the photo she'd taken of the victim's ID and nodded. "Yep, same address."

She rang the bell, and a woman in her sixties answered.

Her cheeks flushed and, with tears in her eyes, she said, "Hello, can I help?"

Sara flashed her warrant card. "DI Sara Ramsey, and this is my partner, DS Carla Jameson. Are you Mrs Rogers?"

"Oh my, yes, yes, I am. Tell me, have you found my daughter?"

"It would be better if we spoke inside, Mrs Rogers. Is your husband home?"

Mrs Rogers backed into the hallway and bellowed for her husband to join her. The entrance consisted of marbled flooring and an oak feature staircase over to the right. Family portraits and photos adorned the walls on this level and swept up the stairs to the top. A lot of the pictures showed the victim. Sara's gut clenched. She knew what lay ahead of her and how tough this news was going to be for the parents to handle.

A tall man in his sixties entered the hallway and stood next to his wife, his face etched with concern. "What's going on here?"

"These ladies are from the police, Doug. It must be about Bonnie." She clung to her husband's arm, and he flung his free one around her shoulders and hugged her to his chest, protectively.

"Do you have some news for us? We've been going out of our minds with worry. Our daughter means everything to us. Have you found her?"

Sara nodded. "I'm sorry to have to report that your daughter's body was found earlier today. She was pulled out of the River Wye by a dog walker."

"No!" Mrs Rogers screamed and collapsed to the cold floor, her husband unable to support her.

He knelt beside her and held her tightly.

He shook his head. "I can't believe this. Bonnie was an excellent swimmer, she would never go near the river, not at this time of the year. Has someone ki... killed her?"

His gaze pierced Sara's soul. "I'm sorry to have to tell you, but yes, that's what we believe, although we'll need to await the pathologist's report from the post-mortem to confirm it. She'll carry that out later today. I'm so sorry for your loss."

"All of this could have been avoided if you had begun the search for our daughter immediately. We knew something dreadful had happened, but your lot refused to take us seriously. This waiting twenty-four-hour rule is bloody absurd, that's what it is. Did she suffer? How did she die? I'm telling you this, you can rule out drowning, she's a stronger swimmer than Rebecca Adlington."

"Like I said, we'll know more after the PM has been

performed. Are you up to answering some questions? If not, we can call back later."

"Come on, love, let's get you onto your feet." He knelt down and hauled his wife up beside him. "We'll go through to the lounge. What sort of questions?"

Sara and Carla followed the distraught couple into a light, bright room that had a fire roaring in the wood-burning stove at the far end. The floor-to-ceiling windows opposite the door showed off a mature shrub-filled garden. A patio area just in front of the window was filled with colourful pots, their flowers either discarded on the paving or drooping, having been battered by the recent heavy rain.

"Take a seat. We'll sit here," Mr Rogers insisted.

He settled his wife in the comfy armchair and sat on the arm. Sara and Carla took a seat on the cream leather couch opposite.

"When you're ready," Mr Rogers prompted, urging Sara to get on with it.

"Bonnie's body was found at Breinton this morning. We're assuming her body was placed in the water further up the river, but that's pure conjecture on our part at this time. Can you tell us the circumstances surrounding your daughter's disappearance?"

"Yes, she was on a night out with friends and didn't come home."

"And what day was this?"

"Tuesday. We knew something was wrong that night, rang the station only to be told to call back the next day. Neither of us slept that night. It was so unlike our daughter not to contact us."

"Did you speak to her friends?"

"Yes, they told us they parted at the taxi rank. Stacey and Tina live in the opposite direction, on the other side of the town. They shared a cab home and left Bonnie waiting for the next car to show up. They regret leaving her alone at the rank, but Bonnie insisted they should get home. That's the type of girl Bonnie was, always putting others first."

"Where had they been on the night out?"

"The three of them had a table booked at the Miller and Carter restaurant in town, and afterwards they stopped off at the Red Admiral just up the road for a few drinks. Are you telling me it's no longer safe for young women to be out at night in this city?"

"It's always advisable to be cautious, whether you're male or female these days. A sign of the times, I'm afraid."

"Is that down to the lack of police out there patrolling our streets? Or more down to the fact that we have some very angry people walking amongst us in Hereford?"

"Possibly a mixture of the two. We're doing our very best to combat the issues, sir."

"Not good enough if our daughter was kidnapped and killed by someone," he shouted, his anger showing in his cheeks.

"I agree, sometimes our hands are tied. I don't suppose you have the contact details of Stacey and Tina, do you? I think we should have a chat with them, see if they can tell us if anything out of the ordinary happened while they were together that night."

Mrs Rogers left her seat and returned with her phone that she withdrew from her handbag close to the fire. "Here's Stacey's number."

Carla stood and noted down the details. Mrs Rogers scrolled further and showed Carla the details for Tina as well, which her partner jotted down before returning to her seat.

"Thank you. Did Bonnie have a boyfriend?" Sara asked.

The distraught couple stared at each other and shook their heads.

"We have to tell them," Mr Rogers whispered.

"It's up to you," his wife said, her voice equally low.

"What's that?" Sara asked.

"She used to go out with a guy called Lee Davison."

"Used to? When did they stop seeing each other? And was the split amicable?"

"Back in the summer, maybe around June," Mr Rogers said. "Amicable? That's debatable. He used to sit outside for hours until she finally gave in and spoke to him. Always ended up in a slanging match after she went out there. I told her to report him to the police for harassing her, but she didn't want the hassle. Ended up taking it out on us, told us to either keep our noses out or she would leave home for good... and now she has."

Mrs Rogers hugged her husband. "Don't go blaming yourself, this has nothing to do with us, Doug."

"Your wife is right, Mr Rogers, there's no point reflecting and wishing you'd handled a situation differently."

"In your professional opinion," he replied tersely.

"It's all I've got to go on," Sara said with a smile.

"Please, Doug, don't start. The officer is only trying to help us. Don't let this become a battle of wills."

"I won't. I'm hurting, the same as you are. All I'm searching for, dear, are answers."

"As are we, Mr Rogers, I can assure you," Sara said.

"You should be out there looking for the loopy individual who took our daughter's life, not sitting here asking your inane questions."

"I'm sorry you feel that way. Bonnie is a stranger to us. In order for us to begin the investigation into her death, it's imperative that we find out about Bonnie and her personality. If she's had any issues or problems with anyone lately, that sort of thing."

"Someone who is likely to want to hurt her? Yes, that

dickhead of an ex of hers, that's who you should be picking up and banging up in a cell. Oh, and you can do us all a favour and throw away the key while you're at it. He's a nasty, scheming waste of space, that one. I can tell you, I raised a glass or two the day she told me she'd finished with him. Scum of the earth, he is. Disrespecting bloody git."

"Now, Doug, don't you go getting worked up again, you know what the doctor has said about your blood pressure."

He wrenched his hand away from his wife and stood, paced the floor back and forth a few times, then sat again with a thud. "I'm sorry. That guy winds me up something chronic. I'd happily wring his neck, given the chance."

"I'll pretend I didn't hear that, Mr Rogers. Can you give us his full name and address?"

"With pleasure. Come on, Lisa, you've got it in your phone still, haven't you?"

"Yes, just a second."

Carla shot out of her seat and again wrote down the details. "Thanks." She returned to sit next to Sara and angled her notebook for her to view it.

"I know where that is," Sara said. "We'll visit him after we leave here, if he's home. I don't suppose you know where he works, do you?"

"Yep, he'll probably be there, not at home. He works at Minor Metals on the edge of town. He's a welder there."

"Interesting. Thanks for your help. Is there anyone else or anything else that has taken place in Bonnie's life recently, in the last six months or so, that has caused you any form of anxiety, or her for that matter?"

The couple stared at each other and eventually shook their heads.

"No, nothing else, only that prick," Doug replied.

"Doug, don't use that language in front of ladies, I've warned you about that before."

"I'm sorry. But that guy boils my bloody piss, has done so on many occasions, and he deserves what's coming to him."

Sara raised her finger. "A word of caution, Mr Rogers, we won't be arresting him, not without any evidence. All we're obliged to do right now is interview him and verify any alibis he has for the time she went missing."

"And what if he put someone up to it? Got someone else to carry out his dirty work for him?"

"We're experienced officers, sir, we can generally tell when someone is pulling the wool over our eyes."

"I didn't mean to suggest otherwise."

His wife gripped his hands. "Let the police do their job, Doug. I don't want all this extra aggravation. I need to grieve the loss of our daughter. I can't do that and manage your temper outbursts at the same time."

"I'm sorry. But you know how much that guy winds me up."

"I do."

"Where did Bonnie work?" Sara asked.

"She didn't. She was at university, she was due to start her final year of Psychology next week. That's why the girls went out because neither Stacey nor Tina could make it any other time before Bonnie returned to Newcastle."

"Is that where Bonnie was studying? Newcastle?"

"That's right. Her dream was to become a psychologist in the future. She had good grades and was well thought of by her lecturers," Mr Rogers said, his eyes filling up with fresh tears.

Sara stalled for a second or two, unsure what to say next. "What about other boyfriends or friends she might have fallen out with lately?"

"No one else. She wasn't the type. She's held on to the same friends since her primary school days. That's why Lee's got to be your main suspect, I know he's mine," Mr Rogers said adamantly.

His wife dug him in the ribs, and he yelped.

"What? I'm just saying. I wouldn't have my eye on anyone else if I were a copper."

"Thank you, Mr Rogers, we'll definitely chase it up, I promise. Is there anything else you can tell us?"

"No, nothing. You need to leave and arrest that bastard before he goes out and finds another victim."

"Doug, what have I told you...? Enough!" Mrs Rogers left her chair, sobbing, and exited the room.

A sheepish Mr Rogers faced them and apologised. "I'm sorry. I let my anger get the better of me. I'm sure you can understand the emotional turmoil I'm going through right now."

"We do. Go, see to your wife, we'll leave you to it. Again, our condolences for your loss. We'll see ourselves out."

"Thank you. I have faith that you will do the right thing, Inspector."

Sara left a business card on the coffee table. "Get in touch if you need me. I'll try and update you as often as I can, but my priority will be hunting down the person responsible for your daughter's death."

"Thank you." He flew out of the room after his wife.

"Come on," Sara said, "let's get out of here before it all kicks off again."

NEXT STOP, they called at the metal factory, but Lee Davison was out at the time. Rather than wait around and waste the next couple of hours, Sara decided to give Stacey and Tina a call. Stacey was free to see them and worked at an estate agency in the centre of Hereford. Sara pulled up outside and waved at the young woman who was expecting them. She came out to see them and climbed into the back of the car.

"Hi, you wanted to see me about Bonnie. Is she okay?"

Sara twisted in her seat to look Stacey in the eye when she broke the sad news. "I'm so sorry, Stacey. Bonnie's body has been found."

"Oh shit! What are you telling me, that she's dead?"

"Unfortunately, yes."

Stacey covered her face with her shaking hands and broke down. "No, this can't be right. Not Bonnie."

"I'm afraid she's been formally identified. We had to break the news to her parents. They informed us that you and Tina were out with Bonnie the night she went missing. Are you up to speaking with us? We have a few questions regarding that night."

"I don't know. Her death has hit me hard. God, how did she die? Can you tell me? Christ, it wasn't the taxi driver, was it? Fuck!"

"We don't know it was him, yet. We'll know more when we receive the post-mortem report, which should come through later today. Her parents told us that you and Tina left her standing at the rank, is that correct?"

She glanced up, and her mouth dropped open then slammed shut again. "You're not suggesting that she died because we left her alone, are you?"

Sara tutted. "No, and I apologise if that's how it came across, that wasn't my intention. Before you separated, did anything untoward happen during the evening?"

Stacey closed her eyes and sighed. "Yes, at the pub. We ran into that fucker... her ex-boyfriend."

"Lee Davison?"

"You know about him?"

"We know of him. Bonnie's parents gave us a brief

rundown of their relationship. Care to tell us more? Was Bonnie scared of him?"

"More than that, she was terrified of him. We all are. He's got several screws loose."

"Was he with anyone else that night?"

"No, he was drinking at the bar, alone, like the saddo he is. He saw us, watched us walk in and take a seat at the table. He turned on his stool and kept staring at us. The guy behind the bar tapped me on the shoulder when I nipped to the loo and asked me if we felt uncomfortable. I told him yes, but what could be done about it? The barman told me that he would deal with the issue and asked Lee to leave. He was seething, threw a few punches, and in the end two members of staff plus a couple of male customers lent a hand and forced him to go."

"Oh heck, did he hang around?"

"Yes, he stood outside for ages, peering through the window at us. The barman came over to check if we were okay, and Bonnie started crying. We couldn't leave, even if we wanted to; we didn't want to take the risk of running into him outside."

"So what did you do?"

"It was all getting too much for Bonnie. The barman came over, asked if we wanted to call the police, but Bonnie pleaded with him not to. She felt it would only make the situation much worse. I agreed with her, knowing how unstable he was. Anyway, another ten minutes, and we glanced up to see that he'd gone. The barman noticed and went to the door to have a look. He confirmed he saw him at the end of the road. We all breathed a sigh of relief. The kind barman then bought us all another drink. He also advised us not to leave for a good half an hour or more. We thanked him for his assistance. He brought the drinks over and said when we wanted to leave, he'd let us out the back way, which led to the taxi rank. That's where we parted. I thought she'd be safe. I've been kicking myself ever since, haven't bloody slept a wink for two nights. Shit, if he did this… there was no one else around that night, it's got to be him. It just has to be."

"Okay, try and remain calm. We know where he works and where he lives, we just needed to get more information about what went on that evening from either you or Tina."

"He's a vile creature. Worse day ever when she started going out with him."

"How long did they date?"

"A couple of years. He started off okay but then he began telling her who she could see, what he wanted her to wear. Used to pull his hair out every time she packed her bags and took off for Newcastle. She told me he would ring her three or four times a day, even during the night sometimes. And, get this, he even showed up at her dorm a few times. I think that got to her the most, him cramping her style, not allowing her any freedom. She waited until she came home one weekend and dumped him. He kicked up a right stink. Fortunately, Bonnie told him outside her house, and when he shouted and made a commotion in the street, her father went out there and told him to back off. There was no love lost between them. I think her father recognised what type of foul-mouthed goon he was after a few months. I know it caused problems between Bonnie and her parents."

"That must have been awful for Bonnie to contend with at times. I'm glad she was able to confide in you."

"Me, too. Tina and I told her more times than I care to remember what a bastard he was and to get rid of him, but deep down I think she was too bloody scared to show him the door."

"What changed her mind?"

"Him showing up at the dorm one day. She was outside, on the steps, chatting to a male student. He saw her and went absolutely nuts. Decked the guy and slapped her several times until a couple of lecturers appeared and ordered him to leave the grounds. He drove home that day and had the nerve to show up when she came home that weekend. She refused to go out with him and ended it there and then. Her father was watching the proceedings, ready to step in and call the police, but Bonnie handled it well and he drove off, never to be seen or heard from again... until Tuesday night."

"How awful. Sounds like she was well rid of him," Sara admitted.

"But at what cost, if he's killed her?"

"We don't know that he has yet. We're definitely going to regard him as a person of interest, at least until we speak to him. Do you know if he's got a police record?"

"I'm not sure. If he has, then Bonnie didn't mention it. But I wouldn't be surprised, he's pretty keen on lashing out first and asking questions later. His type are always in trouble with the cops, right?"

"More often than not. We'll do a background search on him. You never saw him again that night? Not lingering on a street corner or close to the taxi rank perhaps?"

Stacey stared at her and said, "You seriously think we would have left her alone that night if we had?"

"No, I guess you wouldn't have. Is there anything else you think we should know about Lee?"

"Other than he's a frigging tosspot, no, I can't think of anything. I'm sure it won't take you long to suss him out. He's a creep and he makes women's skin crawl."

"Did you have any other problems that night?"

Stacey didn't take the time to consider the question. She shook her head right away. "No, nothing. After we arrived at the pub, we spent most of the time sitting on the edge of our seats because of that bastard staring at us until it kicked off."

"Okay, we'll head over and have a chat with Lee, see what he has to say about the events that evening."

"Ha, I bet he won't admit it. Don't forget to call at the pub, they'll back up our claims. I noticed there were cameras dotted all about the bar. I know how much you guys rely on them to help solve a case."

Sara smiled. "We do. As the saying goes, the camera never lies. We'll certainly follow up on that. Do you think Tina's account will be the same?"

"Yes, we've spoken about it since. Neither of us was drunk, if that's what you're asking. God, I can't believe I'm sitting here, knowing that I'll never lay eyes on Bonnie again. We've been friends since we started playschool together, best friends from the word go. Tina joined us a few weeks later. We had an unbreakable bond that has seen us through a lot of shit over the years, I can tell you."

"Such as?"

"The usual, nothing along the lines of what happened with Lee. None of our other boyfriends behaved like he did once they were dumped, that's what I was getting at."

"Ah, I see. Sorry to be the bearer of such bad news. Is there anything you want to ask us before we leave?"

"When do you think it would be an appropriate time to ring her parents to offer my condolences?"

"Maybe leave it a day or two. Thanks for speaking with us, Stacey. Take care of yourself."

"In other words, I should be looking over my shoulder every time I go out from now on, is that it? Bloody hell, what a shitty society we live in."

"Maybe just keep your wits about you, it can't harm in the future."

"I swear I'm never going near another bloke as long as I live if a relationship can turn out the way Bonnie's did. It's enough to put you off men for bloody life."

Sara nodded, and her gaze drifted to Carla who hadn't said a word during the interview.

"Not all men are bad, just remember that."

Stacey left the car.

"Jesus, I know how she feels." Carla sighed. "How did I ever learn to trust another man?"

"He's one of us, that's how. You struck lucky when you met Des. He's a good man, especially when you compare him to the other fucker who blighted your life."

"Yeah, I know. But the thought was there all the same, that I shouldn't trust another man again. Jesus, she's right, most women I know will spend the rest of their lives looking over their shoulders when they're out alone. We're screwed. Why should it be that way? Why can't we have the freedom to enjoy ourselves just like men?"

"I don't know the answer to that, love. Maybe self-defence classes should be introduced to the school curricula, if only to furnish young women with a feeling of empowerment that will combat issues in later life."

Carla's eyes widened. "Yeah, okay, if you say so."

"Right, I'm probably talking a load of crap, as usual. I'm thinking it won't be worth going to speak with Tina but I am getting anxious about interviewing Davison now."

"What's the answer?"

"I'm going to call for backup, get either Craig or Barry to come and join us before we visit the metal factory again."

"Makes sense. Do you want me to return to the station?"

"No, tag along for the ride. It won't hurt to go in there as a threesome."

"If nothing else it'll let him know we mean business. What about asking the team to go over the footage of any cameras in the area around the pub? And don't forget we should call in and have a word with the barman, get his side of the events."

"I knew there was a reason I like having you as my partner." Sara reached for her phone and contacted the team. "Ah, Barry, just the person I needed to have a word with. Fancy joining us?"

"Boss? Name the time and the place, and I'll be there."

"At Minor Metals in about an hour. Carla and I have another stop to make first."

"I'll be there."

"Can you also arrange to obtain any footage in the area of Miller and Carter and the Red Admiral pub from Tuesday night? We're going to pop along and have a chat with the staff at the pub now."

"I'm trying to think of what cameras are in that part of town, and I think there are only a few, but I'll do my best."

"What about around the taxi rank?" Carla suggested.

"Yes, that's a good call. Did you get that, Barry?"

"I did, boss. I'll get the camera genius on it."

"I thought you might. See you in an hour."

"Rightio."

Sara ended the call. "Talking about taxis, it might be worth going down to the rank, see if we can locate the driver, get his spin on things."

"I was about to propose the same. Why don't you call Barry back, get him to do a detour on his way to the factory? It'll save us rushing while we conduct the interviews at the pub."

Sara winked at her partner. "Yet another fine idea." She rang Barry back and issued the instructions which he was only too happy to instigate.

THE PUB WAS FILLING up nicely as it was close to lunchtime.

"Christ, where does the day go?" Sara said.

"We've had an exceptionally busy morning, and it isn't over yet," Carla confirmed.

There was an older man and a younger woman serving behind the bar.

Sara approached the man and flashed her warrant card. "Hi, is the manager around?"

"You're looking at him. What can I do for you?"

"We were hoping to have a quiet word with you."

He spread his hand across the bar. "You'd be better off coming back at around three in that case. Sorry, we're about to get snowed under."

"I can see. Okay, don't worry."

"Unless... wait a second." He raced across to an opening behind the bar and bellowed for Dan to join him.

A young man appeared and wiped his hands down his already grubby jeans.

"Get washed up and stand in for me for ten minutes, will you, mate?"

"Sure, Chris. I'll be right back."

The barman returned. "I can spare you ten minutes. Can I get you ladies a drink? It'll be on the house."

"Two orange juice would be great, thanks very much."

"Take a seat over by the window, I'll be with you shortly."

Sara led the way through the crowded tables to the only available table left on offer. "I didn't even know this place existed. I feel like I'm missing out."

"I've been here a few times. The food is good. It's a bit quieter in the evenings."

"Get you. I'll crawl back in my cave. I feel like a bloody dinosaur."

Chris joined them a few minutes later, once the younger guy had taken over the reins behind the bar. "Now, what can I do for you, ladies?"

Sara sipped at her OJ. "We were hoping you might be able to help us with our enquiries regarding an incident that occurred on your premises a few days ago. Tuesday evening to be precise."

"I know the incident you're talking about. The guy sat at the bar who was harassing the three women. I was one of those who kicked him out, slimeball. I have a reputation to uphold. Lots of ladies come here because they consider it a safe place for them to hang out. I cottoned on right away to what he was up to. He was keen on intimidating them, so I asked him to leave. Of course, I checked with the girls first, in case I was misreading the signs. Turns out my gut feeling was correct. Why do you want to know, has something happened?"

Sara inhaled and exhaled a breath to calm her racing pulse. "Yes, unfortunately, the body of a young woman was pulled from the river this morning. She was his ex-girlfriend, the one he was harassing on Tuesday evening."

He ran a hand through his short, cropped hair. "Jesus Christ, what the hell! And you suspect he's the one who killed her? Was she killed? Or did she die of natural causes? Nah, don't answer that, too much of a coincidence after what took place that evening. Bugger. How can I help?"

"I don't suppose you have any CCTV cameras focused on the bar area, do you?"

He tapped the side of his nose. "I'm with you. Grab your drinks and come with me to my office. I'll have to make it snappy, though, the kitchen is about to get inundated with orders, and if I don't chip in and ensure things run smoothly, I'll end up giving away more than I take because of complaints."

"I'm with you. We can call back later, it's no problem."

"No, let's get you sorted now. If I don't deal with things as they happen, I have a habit of getting overwhelmed with chores."

The three of them left the bar area, and Chris showed them through to his tiny office.

"It's a bit cramped but serviceable. Tuesday around tennish if I remember rightly."

"That's fantastic, we weren't sure what time the incident took place."

"I'm not likely to forget it. I've still got a couple of sore ribs causing me aggro. He was a feisty shit." He focused on swapping the discs over and running through the footage on the new one he'd inserted. "Here we go. This is where the three girls enter. He's already sitting on the stool at the bar. Fuck, the way he's watching them, it's even making *me* want to vomit. I hadn't noticed that at first. There I am, behind the bar, working my socks off as usual. I believe we were short-staffed that night. I think I realised what was going on about here because I couldn't take my eyes off him after that." He flicked to another camera angle which highlighted the victim and her two friends. "You can see how anxious the girls are getting. They tried to ignore him at first."

Carla shuddered. "Creepy. Why didn't they up and leave?"

"Maybe they thought they'd be safer dealing with the letch in a public place," Sara suggested.

"What an absolute scumbag. He's giving me the creeps, just watching his ruddy antics," Carla replied.

"Yeah, we all agree it's not how men should react. I'm glad I've seen the footage before we head over and question him," Sara said, unable to take her eyes off the screen. "I don't suppose you have time to run us off a copy, do you, Chris?"

"Yes, it shouldn't take long, I'm happy to oblige."

THEY LEFT THE PUB, disc in hand, five minutes later.

"Let's head over to the factory," Sara said. "Hopefully Barry will be there by now. Perhaps he'll have some news for us regarding the taxi drivers or the cameras in situ around the rank."

"We can but hope."

"What's wrong? You sound a bit down." As soon as the question left her mouth, Sara could have kicked herself. "Sorry, forget I asked. Are you all right?"

"I'm fine. Things like this are bound to affect me. I suppose it just brings it home to me how lucky I was to escape *his* clutches."

Sara grabbed Carla's hand and squeezed it. "You were. You saw the light early enough to do something about it, love. Have you heard from him since? Or seen him when you've been out on the town?"

"No, thank goodness. Maybe he moved away from the area. I dread to think how my life would have turned out had I stuck with him." Tears welled up, and Carla swiped them away with the cuff of her jacket. "I don't know what I would have done if you hadn't intervened. Been there for me when I needed to vent."

"Hush now. There's no need for you to get upset, it's all in the past. I'll always be here for you, Carla. We're a team, and a damn good one to boot."

They shared an awkward hug over the centre console, and Sara patted her on the back.

"Now get a grip, we have a suspect to interview."

"I'm okay. He sounds a right charmer. I wonder what she saw in him. No, no, forget I said that."

Sara laughed and started the engine. They drove through the heavy traffic and pulled up outside the factory fifteen minutes later to find Barry parked up, awaiting their arrival. He jumped into the back seat.

"Hey, how did you get on?" Sara asked.

"There are a few cameras near the rank, and a couple more

up the road for us to have a look at. I questioned some of the drivers stationed down there at the time, but none of them were on duty that night. They advised me to go back in the evening to have a word with the drivers who do the night shift."

Sara nodded. "Might not be a bad idea. I suppose it's logical. You wouldn't work day and night around here. Might be different if this was a tourist area."

"I agree," Barry said. "I don't mind volunteering to spend half an hour or more interviewing the drivers who were on duty around the time the girls needed the taxis. Do we know what time that was?"

"I'll give Stacey a call, I forgot to ask," Sara admitted.

"If you go by the footage we've obtained from the pub," Carla began, "Davison was kicked out at about ten."

"That's true. Let me give Stacey a call to get confirmation." Sara opened up her notebook and punched Stacey's number into her phone. "Hi, Stacey, sorry, it's me again, DI Sara Ramsey. Can you talk?"

"Er... yes. What's wrong?"

"Nothing's wrong, I just wanted to check with you what time you caught the taxi home on Tuesday? Sorry, I should have asked you earlier, it slipped my mind."

"Gosh, now you're asking. I think it must have been around ten-forty-five or eleven."

"Would Tina know?"

"No, she's hopeless with details like that."

"Never mind. We'll see what we can find on the nearby cameras."

"Oh, that's an excellent idea. Are there a lot in the area?"

"A few. Thanks again for taking my call. How are you bearing up?"

"I'm still in shock. I had a word with my boss, and he's told me that I can go home early if I need to. But what will I do at home? Stew over it. It wouldn't be right letting everyone down here."

"I can understand your logic. Thanks again. Take care of yourself."

"Thank you, I hope you find out what happened to Bonnie."

"I have every confidence we will." Sara ended the call. "Between ten-forty-five and eleven, Barry."

"That'll make it easier, narrowing the time down like that. Speaking to the other drivers, they said any fares they pick up from the rank aren't registered anywhere, unlike those that come from the control room."

Sara chewed on her lip. "I hadn't considered that aspect. Ugh... not what we wanted to hear, eh? Oh well, let's see what the cameras can tell us. Maybe one of the drivers will remember her and be able to give us some kind of feedback further down the line. Until then, we'll see what Lee Davison has to say for himself." She glanced at the clock on the dashboard and opened the door. "It's time."

The reception area was quite small compared to others Sara had seen lately at some of the factories they'd needed to visit in the area, on official business.

A brunette wearing spectacles with her hair done up in a bun on the top of her head glanced up from her paperwork and approached the counter. "Ah, you've returned to see Lee Davison. I didn't get a chance to tell him you wanted to speak to him because his supervisor was waiting to see him about a problem they have on the line."

Sara smiled and nodded. "That's okay. Will he be free to see us now?"

"Possibly. I'll check." She marched off through an open doorway and returned a few minutes later.

Sara studied her mannerisms and didn't like what was on show. "Is there a problem?"

"Yes, umm… oh, I don't know how to say this."

"Just spitting it out quickly would be advisable."

"I told him the police were here to see him, and he took off."

"What? Shit, which way did he go?"

The receptionist gulped and was on the verge of tears. Nervously, she ran a hand over her face. "Out to the car park," she whispered.

Sara didn't respond. She turned and ran out of the main entrance with Barry and Carla behind her, but Barry soon charged ahead of her once they were out in the open. A car revved its engine and drove at them at full pelt. Barry shoved Sara out of the way, but it was too late for Carla. The car's tyres squealed, and gravel scattered, smashing Sara in the face and upper body. She shielded her head to prevent further damage and at the same time shouted for Carla to jump back.

However, much to Sara's dismay, her partner remained pinned in the same position, frozen to the spot. Barry bounced to his feet to try to save Carla. Everything happened in slow motion and yet so quickly, much to Sara's horror.

The car hit her partner at speed, sending Carla flying over the bonnet and the roof and then slamming her into the boot of the BMW. Sara stared after the car, anchored to the spot herself. That was until she heard Barry talking to the operator and asking for an ambulance.

"Carla! No!" *She can't be dead, she can't be.*

CHAPTER 5

Sara buried her head in her hands, Barry's arm looped around her shoulder.

"She can't die. Why aren't they doing something to save her?"

"They're getting the equipment prepared, boss. We need to hang tight and keep everything crossed that Carla is going to pull through. Shit, should I give Des a ring?"

"Yes, yes, we should do that, he should be here with her. Hearing his voice might bring her round."

Barry removed his arm and dug his phone out of his pocket. "I need to speak with DI Des Williams. Yes, it's an urgent matter. This is DC Barry Thomas."

Barry tapped his foot and then began pacing back and forth in front of Sara until she held out a hand and caught his forearm.

"You're making me dizzy."

"Sorry, ma'am, I'm nervous about making the call."

Sara snatched the phone out of his hand. "Leave it to me." It was her turn to tap her foot, waiting for Des to answer the damn phone.

"Barry, what's up?"

"It's not Barry. Des, it's me, Sara Ramsey, there's been an accident..."

"My God, is Carla all right?"

"The honest answer is, I don't know. The paramedics are here, working on her."

"Working on her? Shit, I'm on my way, where are you?"

The sound of his chair scraping filled the line—well, that and the odd cuss word said under his breath.

"We're at Minor Metals, a factory out near Credenhill, do you know it?"

"No, but I'll ask around before I set off. No bullshit, Sara, how bad is she?"

Sara's throat clogged up, and she coughed to clear it. "Pretty bad, not that I'm any kind of medical expert. Just get here, Des, and promptly."

"Leaving now. If you get the chance, tell her I love her."

"I will. Drive carefully."

"See you soon."

Des ended the call, and Sara's courage gave way to despondency. Her gaze flitted between the motionless body of Carla lying in a twisted heap on the road and Barry who appeared to be equally as shell-shocked as she was.

"Hey, we've got to think positive... for her sake. Jesus, why did this have to happen? Barry, come on, we need to snap out of this, let the professionals do their jobs. The suspect has got away. It's imperative that we track the fucker down. Ring the station, get every available car searching for this mongrel. Circulate his plate number. Let's get the arsehole before he's got the chance to abscond and possibly leave the county."

Barry shook out his arms and reclaimed his phone from Sara. He stepped away and turned his back on the scene to allow himself the focus he needed to make the call. When he returned to stand alongside Sara, the poor constable was shaking uncontrollably.

"Are you okay?"

"Not really, but I'll survive. How are things going?"

"It's hard to say. They've done CPR on her and rigged her up to the machines now. I think her heart is pumping, but that's about all." The emotions swept through her very core and overwhelmed her. "Shit! She can't die. I need her by my side."

"There's one thing going in her favour, she's a fighter. We have to believe she's got it in her to pull through this. She has everyone behind her, I'm sure that will help."

Sara smiled at Barry. Bless him, he was doing all he could to keep her spirits up and not making a lot of sense in the process. Tyres screeched behind them, and a car door slammed. Sara spun on the spot to see Des tearing towards them, his gaze trained on the two paramedics trying to perform a miracle on his fiancée.

"Jesus. Is she okay? What the fuck happened here?"

Her voice trembling, along with the rest of her body, Sara recounted what had taken place.

"What? And you let the fucker get away? Sorry, that came out wrong. Of course your priority would lie with Carla, but, man… he needs to be caught and go down for this, Sara."

"I know, you don't have to drum it into me, Des. There's an alert out for the suspect, that's as much as we can do right now."

Des kicked out at a nearby stone and watched it spin off towards one of the parked cars. "Shit! Why her? She can't bail out on me, not now. Bloody hell, I love that woman so much. I need her to survive, Sara, my life won't be worth living. I mean, I'll be a lost soul without her. She means absolutely everything and more to me."

"I know. That's how I feel. She's more than a partner to

me, always has been." Sara left her position, finally plucking up the courage to approach the paramedics. "How is she? And I need you to be truthful, not tell me what you think I want to hear."

"We managed to get her heart going again but, in all honesty, it's going to be touch and go. She has youth on her side, that's as much as we can say for now. We're preparing to move her, to transfer her to hospital. We'll know more once a doctor takes a look at her."

"Okay, thank you. Please, do your best for her," Sara pleaded.

"Don't worry," the male paramedic replied, his brow wrinkled with concern.

"I'm her fiancé, can I come with her?" Des said, his voice strained.

"Of course, we'll give you the nod when we're ready to go."

Des and Sara took a step back, allowing the paramedics to work swiftly and unhindered.

Sara clutched Des' forearm. "We have to believe she's going to make it. I can't bear to contemplate the alternative."

"Me neither. Christ, I need to contact her parents."

"Maybe leave it a little while, do that at the hospital. They're bound to ask what's going on and, at present, you're unable to tell them."

"Shit, I think they're away at the moment. On holiday abroad somewhere. Shit! What do I do, Sara?"

"Nothing. Not yet. Hang fire until we know more."

"Fuck! Why her? If I get my hands on the fucking scum who deliberately ran her down..."

"Talking like that isn't going to help, Des. We need to remain calm, let the boys out there deal with the bastard. They'll catch him, sooner rather than later. I have every confidence in them."

"I hope you're right. What a fucking wretched individual he must be. Who is he?"

"He's a person of interest in a murder inquiry we're working on. We were about to question him as to his whereabouts on Tuesday, the night he caused aggro with his ex-girlfriend. Her body was found in the river this morning."

"What a screwed-up fucker he must be to take Carla out like that."

"He won't get away with it, I promise, not while I'm in charge of the frigging case."

The paramedics lifted the stretcher into the back of the ambulance.

Sara clutched Des' arm again. "Go with her. Keep talking to her, telling her how much you love her. We'll pull her through this." She leaned over and pecked him on the cheek.

"My car." He handed Sara the keys.

"Leave it with me, either Barry or another member of the team will take care of it. That's the least of your worries."

"Thanks, love. I'll keep in touch. As soon as I hear anything, you'll be the first to know."

"I appreciate it. Stay strong. Between us, we've got this. Remember, she's a fighter, she needs us to have the same mindset."

"Don't worry. Speak later."

Sara's heart sank as she watched him get in the back of the ambulance instead of her. She was aware of how selfish her thoughts were and shook her head to disperse them.

"Are you okay? Or is that a futile question?" Barry asked.

Sara offered him a weak smile. "I think you know the answer to that. I'm mortified I'm not going with her but I know she's in safe hands. Here are the keys of Des' car. You drive it back to the station, and I'll follow you."

"Don't jump on me, but are you okay to drive, boss? This has all been a huge shock for you."

"I'll be okay. Let's get going. We need to bring the team up to date, and I want a chat with the desk sergeant ASAP to emphasise how important it is that we nail this bastard."

SARA BLOCKED out the image of Carla flying through the air and landing on the road, at least she tried to, but every time she braked during the journey to the station, the image came hurtling back to haunt her. "Get a grip, girl. I'm going to be no use to anyone if I don't. The rest of the team are going to be reliant on me to keep things running like clockwork in Carla's absence."

A car blasted her from behind when the lights changed to green and, tempted as she was to give the driver the finger, instead, she waved an apology and drove off.

At the station, Jeff was beside himself. "Dare I ask how she is, ma'am?"

"They're taking care of her, that's about as much as I know. Des is with her. There was little point in both of us being at the hospital with her. How's the hunt going for the bastard who ran her over?"

"It's going. We had a sighting of the vehicle about ten minutes ago but lost him again. I've deployed more cars to the area to join in the search."

"Do your best, Jeff, I know you won't let me down, or Carla come to that."

"I won't, and neither will my team, ma'am. Shocking, we're all devastated but we're determined to make the..." he glanced over his shoulder to check there was no one in earshot and lowered his voice to add, "make the fucker pay."

Sara patted his hand. "I'm glad we're singing from the same song sheet. Keep me updated, if you would?"

"I will. Take care of yourself. She's in safe hands at the hospital."

"I know she is."

Sara trudged her way up the stairs, her legs wearier than she'd ever known them. Barry had gone on ahead and had a mug of coffee ready and waiting for her.

"Cheers, mate. Have you brought the team up to date?"

"I did. Sorry if I've overstepped the mark, boss."

"You haven't. Don't ever think that. Look, while Carla's out of action, I'm going to need a temporary partner. Do you think you can handle it?"

He prodded at his chest. "Me? I don't know. I think so, boss."

"Of course he can handle it," Craig shouted from across the far side of the room.

The rest of the team all agreed, and Barry's cheeks flared.

"I guess, in that case, the decision has already been made for me. What do you need me to do next, boss?"

"Carry on with what we've already got on the table for now. If I have to go out for any reason, I'll give you a shout. Craig, tell me you've got some news regarding the cameras."

"I've found a couple of things I think you should look at."

Sara walked towards him. "Show me. Barry, do you want to join us?"

Sara and Barry stood either side of Craig. He opened up a couple of screens on his computer and positioned them side by side.

"Here we have two different cars and two vans which appeared to slow down while they drove past the girls as they walked towards the taxi rank on Tuesday."

He played the footage, and Sara nodded.

"I agree, it certainly seems that way. Can you focus on the registration numbers?"

"I've got three out of the four vehicles so far. The final one, this van here, is proving to be a little more difficult to track down."

"Sounds suspicious, as though we should be throwing all our efforts at that van, but what if it backfires on us and the driver turns out to be innocent?" She placed her finger and thumb on either side of her chin. "We should keep our options open, shouldn't we?" she asked her two colleagues, suddenly doubting herself.

"I agree," Barry said. "Want me to lend Craig a hand? Two heads are better than one and all that."

"Yes, do that. I'll be in my office. Wait, did one of the cars belong to Lee Davison?"

Craig shook his head. "No, which kind of surprised me, given what's gone on today."

"Okay, I'm not sure what to make of it all just yet. Call me if you find anything new."

Sara took her mug and walked into her office. She paused to take a few sips of her coffee, her mind whirling, her thoughts lying with Carla and her unenviable position, while she took in the view of the Brecons. Her phone rang. She dashed around the desk to answer it but paused again.

What if it's bad news about Carla? What if...

No, she refused to go down that route.

"DI Sara Ramsey, how can I help?"

"Sara, it's me, Lorraine. Is it true?"

"What? If you're talking about Carla, then yes, the gossip you've heard is true."

"There's no need to take that tone with me. This is the last time I call you and show some concern."

"I'm sorry. I don't know what came over me... no wait, yes I do. I'm going out of my mind with worry. The paramedics managed to get her heart going at the scene. Des is with her at the hospital. I feel totally left out of it. I didn't think it warranted two serving police officers sitting by her side."

"No, I can understand your point of view, but raging rivers and forked lightning wouldn't have kept me away."

"Great, how to make a girl feel ten times worse than she already does."

"Bollocks, I wasn't having a dig at you, I was merely stating facts."

"Well, don't. Des is by her side, he's her fiancé after all. Who am I to argue with his decision? Anyway, I've got a fucking suspect to hunt down and a killer to find. Are the two connected? I don't know, that's another issue blighting my life. Apart from that, yes, everything is simply marvellous."

"I can tell I've caught you at a bad time."

"Bugger, sorry for going off on one. I'm shitting myself here. You didn't see her, she was busted up pretty good, Lorraine. I'm rooting for her, I truly am, but I don't know if she's going to make it."

"She will. She's going to receive expert care at the hospital, you need to cling on to that hope."

"I'm doing my best. Damn, why did it have to be her? Why couldn't it have been me?"

"Now you're just talking utter bullshit. No one knows what's around the corner. If our card is marked then there's very little anyone can do to alter the fact. This isn't like you, Sara. You're one of the most positive people I know."

"I'm struggling, I'll be the first to admit it. And yes, I know I have to kick myself up the arse. I'll do that tonight, if I get the chance."

"Idiot. The only reason I rang up was to tell you that I'm here if you need me. Never think you're alone. I owe you so much, my life for one thing. I'm not about to run out on you when you need someone by your side."

"Thanks, Lorraine. I needed to hear that today. We're all

in this together. It's unbelievably hard to comprehend when one of our own gets taken down."

"Stop talking like that, as though she's not going to make it. She's tougher than you think. Look what she's been through already in life. This will be a breeze for her to recover from in comparison."

"Funny that, we were only speaking about her past upheavals and how she'd overcome them, earlier, and then this fucking happened. You couldn't make it up." Her voice caught in her throat as a lump the size of a watermelon appeared.

"I hear you. Sara, don't crumble, not now. You're far stronger than that. She's going to be relying on your resilience to get her through this, we all are. You're the most remarkable, toughest and capable woman I know. Dig deep, draw on your reserves if you must. And listen to me on this one, you need to delegate more. The team won't mind, they'll need the extra work to occupy their time as well. You're going to need each other to get you through this, the cruellest of times, but knowing you the way I do, you've got this. And here's another thing, you need to call me, reach out to me if you get overwhelmed and think you can't carry on. I know how hard this is going to hit you. Not yet, but in time, it'll grab you round the throat when you least expect it."

"I'll have to take your word for that because I've never experienced anything like this before."

"Utter codswallop... maybe not with a work partner, but are you forgetting what happened to Philip?"

"No, I could never forget that. I meant with a work colleague. She's so much more than just a partner, though."

"I'd be flabbergasted if you didn't think that. She's going to pull through. That needs to be your mantra from now on, promise me."

Sara chuckled, her heart feeling suddenly much lighter,

thanks to her good friend's rallying words. "You're amazing, and after what you've recently been through as well."

"Hey, that's all in the past. And who do I have to thank for coming out the other side relatively unharmed? One Sara Ramsey."

"Get away with you, it was a team effort. You played your part in your own fate as well."

"I know but I'll also forever be in debt to you and Carla, for rescuing and releasing me from the clutches of that madman. I owe you guys one and I intend to deliver when I can."

"Nonsense, it's what friends do for each other, even in the line of duty. Haven't you got work to be getting on with? Umm… sorry, I haven't had a chance to check my emails yet so haven't got a clue if you've sent over your latest report or not."

"Not is the answer. I've had three PMs to perform this morning, therefore the paperwork will have to wait until after I've stuffed my face. Talking of which, have you eaten yet?"

"No. I can't stomach anything. Thanks for being there for me, Lorraine."

"You're most welcome. Ring me anytime, if you're feeling low."

"I will. Thanks, love."

Sara ended the call and addressed some emails she had ignored that morning. With her mind elsewhere, she gave up on that chore a few minutes later and returned to be with her team, needing their presence around her to get her through the rest of the day.

"How are we doing, guys? Has anyone managed to find out if Lee Davison has a police record, yet?" Her gaze drifted over to Christine.

"I have, boss. He's been charged with ABH and GBH, served time for the GBH, minimal sentence of four months."

"Bloody pitiful. How do they expect us to keep this country safe when they dish out piss-poor sentences like that? It was a rhetorical question. Anything against women?"

"Yes, there was an assault charge from a former girlfriend who later dropped the charges."

"Interesting. Does it mention why?"

"It's not on the file, boss. Want me to see if I can track her down?"

"You read my mind, Christine. I'd like a chat with her, even if it's only over the phone."

Christine nodded and went to work on her keyboard while Sara circulated the room. She glanced up a few minutes later to see Christine vying for her attention. She crossed the room to speak with her.

"Have you got it?"

"I have a mobile number for her. I haven't tried it yet."

"Ring it, and I'll speak with her."

Christine made the call and then handed the phone to Sara once it began ringing.

"Hi, is this Kerry Lynch?"

"Yeah, it is. If you're selling something then I ain't interested. There's a frigging cost-of-living crisis going on, and any spare cash I've got I'm using to fund my kid's haul of toys, no offence."

"None taken. I'm DI Sara Ramsey, Kerry. How old is your child?"

"Umm... three, why?"

"Boy or girl?"

"A boy, and I'm making sure he doesn't turn out to be like his father."

"And who might that be? Lee Davison?"

"God, yes. I cringe every time I hear that damn name. What do you want? You didn't say."

"Some information, if I may?"

"About?"

"Your child's father."

"He's not, it takes a real man to be called a father. Let's call him a sperm donor, and even that goes against the grain."

"I totally get that after what he did to you. Is your son the result of his assault?"

"Yes. He's part of me, hence the reason I didn't choose to terminate him. It doesn't stop me wondering if he carries the bad genes of his... father."

"A tough call to make. Can you tell me what happened? Or more to the point why you dropped your claim against Davison?"

"Because I found out I was pregnant. He doesn't know. I couldn't take the risk of turning up in court with a bump. I'd never get rid of the bastard then, would I? Why are you ringing me?"

"Unfortunately, he caused problems with his ex on Tuesday while she was out with friends, and something happened to her in the days since then."

"Eh? What are you trying to say? Don't tell me he's done something daft like kidnap her?"

Sara thought that was a strange comment for Kerry to say out of the blue. "Why would you ask that?"

Kerry fell quiet.

"Kerry, did he threaten to kidnap you?"

"Yes. Quite a few times. It was either that or he warned me that my family members would be at risk..."

"At risk?"

"If I didn't continue going out with him. To share his bed with him."

"Shit! How long did you allow this kind of behaviour to

go on?" Sara bit down on her tongue and squeezed her eyes shut for coming right out with what sounded to her ears like an accusation.

"Don't judge me, please, I can hear it in your tone. Unless you've ever been in a similar situation, you're wrong to think badly of the decisions I was forced to make at the time." Kerry began crying. "I hate myself for allowing him to touch me, every night for weeks, for months. But what the fuck was I supposed to do when he was threatening to carry out all sorts on my two kid sisters and my own mother?"

"I'm sorry, I was in the wrong. I'm not judging you. It's regrettable that you didn't follow through with the charge you raised against him."

"I know that now, after what you've just told me. I'm sorry he hounded his ex-girlfriend. I hope nothing came of it, for her sake."

Sara swallowed down the acid burning her constricted throat. "I have to tell you that her body was found this morning."

Kerry gasped. "Holy shit! Seriously? Are you telling me that he went ahead and killed her?"

Sara tutted and blew out a frustrated breath. "We really don't have any evidence to prove that's the case. All we're going on is supposition right now. But we're searching for any possible clues that will put him in the frame for the crime. I'm trusting this won't go any further. You told me you're not in contact with him, is that correct?"

"Yes. Bloody hell, I would never call him to warn him the police were on his tail, especially not after the way he treated me. Shit. That poor woman. Did she suffer? Sounds to me like all his threats have come to fruition."

"Possibly. I also stated that without evidence we can't pin anything on him as yet."

"You need to work harder then, because take my word for

it, he's bloody capable of doing all that and more. I wouldn't put it past him to try and take someone's life if he's pushed hard enough. Why do you think I left Hereford with my kid, his son?"

"I get that. Are you somewhere safe? Where he can't find you?"

"I believe so. Let's just say he hasn't managed to track me down so far."

"All right. Can you note down my name and number and get in touch if the situation changes?"

"God, please don't say that. I couldn't bear to live on tenterhooks for the rest of my life. You must capture him and quickly. He's dangerous, surely you realise that by now."

Sara didn't have the heart to reveal what had happened to Carla, to back up the claim she was making. "I assure you, we're doing our very best. Take care. Promise me you'll keep your wits about you for the foreseeable future."

"I will. Good luck with finding him. He deserves to be behind bars, even if it turns out that he hasn't killed his ex. He's a danger to society, and women in particular."

"I agree. Ring me if you need me." Sara ended the call and exhaled the stale breath burning her lungs. She handed the phone back to Christine. "Poor woman is beside herself. The need to find Davison has quadrupled. She's right about one thing… he's a danger to society. If he can take down a police officer on duty without blinking an eye, then we seriously have to consider what else he's capable of doing."

"You're not wrong, boss. Is there anything I can do?"

"Apart from all of us leaving the office and jumping in our cars to help search for the bastard, no. I think we're up to scratch on his background information, we just need to find the fucker and then throw everything we've got at him."

She walked across the room and spent the next ten minutes bringing the whiteboard up to date.

THE GAMES PEOPLE PLAY

Sara was interrupted by Barry shouting, "Boss, they've had another sighting of him. Three cars are chasing him. I don't suppose it'll be long before they capture him."

"Excellent news. Keep me informed, Barry. I'll have everything crossed in the meantime."

It was a full thirty minutes later before they received the news they'd been waiting for; that their main suspect was in custody. The patrol cars had to carry out the dangerous procedure of boxing his vehicle in on the dual carriageway. One of the patrol cars had been forced off the road and had hit a lamppost. The driver and passenger were both on their way to hospital as a precaution after their airbags had been deployed. Davison had been caught on the main road to Worcester; who knows where he might have ended up with the M5 within spitting distance? Sara punched the air and breathed out a sigh of relief once the news broke, although, at the same time, her thoughts lay with the officers who had risked their lives to box the bastard in.

"Thank fuck for that. I can't wait to see what the arsehole has to say for himself during an interview. Barry, I don't want to waste any time when he gets here. Ensure the desk sergeant organises the duty solicitor ASAP."

"On it now, boss."

Sara spent the next five minutes making well-earned coffees for the team while running through the questions she intended firing at Davison once he arrived. The team accepted the drinks on offer, and Sara drifted into her office to jot down some notes before she forgot anything. Ten minutes later, she was notified by the desk sergeant that Davison was standing in reception. She bolted out of her office, notebook in hand, and collected Barry on the way down the stairs to Interview Room One.

Davison had defiance written all over him. He was sitting at the table, a coffee in his hands. Next to him was a duty solicitor who Sara had met a couple of times in the past few months.

"Hello, again, Ms Tyler. Thanks for coming so quickly."

"My pleasure, Inspector. Shall we get started? My client is keen to get out of here."

Sara nodded. "Whatever you wish. Barry, would you get the interview underway?" En route to the interview room she had already primed the constable on what to say.

He started the proceedings like a natural, with no hesitation on his part at all.

Sara flipped open her notebook and asked her first question. "Why did you leave the scene of an accident today?"

Davison's grin displayed crooked yellowing teeth. "No comment."

Sara resisted the temptation to launch herself across the table and slap that smug smirk from his ugly face. Her blood heating up, she concentrated all her efforts on not allowing this fucker to screw with her. "Come now, Mr Davison, we've got you bang to rights on the CCTV footage from the factory. It's going to be a waste of your time, and ours, denying it."

Ms Tyler leaned over and whispered something to her client.

Davison kept his gaze on Sara, refusing to lose eye contact with her. He sat upright and grinned again. "No comment."

"I can see we're not going to get very far with this line of questioning, so I guess we'll see you in court regarding that particular charge. The charge of attempted murder of a police officer." She watched his eyes widen and the colour in his cheeks drain.

"Like fuck. She stood in the way as I was driving off the property."

Sara gave three loud tuts. "Unfortunately, there are two

witnesses in this room who can state otherwise. If it hadn't been for my colleague's foresight in pushing me out of the way, I fear I might have been mown down as well, just like my partner."

"Whatever. No comment."

"How is your partner, Inspector?" Tyler asked.

"I'm afraid we're still awaiting an update on her condition from the hospital. Her fiancé is by her side. He's promised to contact me with any news as it happens. But thank you for asking, I'm glad someone is concerned enough about her."

The solicitor nodded. "I'll hold her in my thoughts and prayers."

Davison swiftly glanced at Tyler and grimaced. "Are you for real?"

Tyler's eyes flickered shut and reopened, but she didn't look at him. Instead, she focused on her A4 notebook.

"You're as bad as they are. Thick as thieves, ain't ya? I want my own solicitor here," Davison demanded.

"As is your right. What's their name?" Sara asked.

"I ain't got one but I'll soon bloody find one."

"Not good enough. We've done our part, Mr Davison, provided you with legal representation. Deal with it."

He sat back and glared at Sara, his hands balling into fists on the table in front of him.

"Moving on. We called at your place of work for a reason today, to interview you as part of an ongoing inquiry. Tell me, why did you feel the need to run from us?"

"I didn't. I was on my way out when you showed up."

Sara inclined her head. "Not according to the receptionist. She informed you that the police were there to see you and, in her words, you ran, or did she use the word bolted? Either way, it amounts to pretty much the same thing, you were keen to avoid speaking with us. May I ask why?"

"I wasn't. I had to leave, I had a dentist's appointment, and the supervisor had already made me late, calling an impromptu meeting with me."

"That sounds to me to be a very convenient excuse. What's the name of your dentist? I'm sure they'll either confirm or deny that you had an appointment with them today."

"Whatever… sorry, I mean, no comment."

Again, the urge to strike the bastard was proving too powerful to resist, but she managed it, just.

Tyler jumped in with a question of her own. "May I ask why you wished to speak with my client in the first place, Inspector?"

"You may. It was to do with an incident that happened on Tuesday night. Oh, sorry, you won't be aware of this, Ms Tyler, let me fill you in. Your client was, how shall I put this…? Causing mischief with an ex-girlfriend of his which resulted in him being thrown out of a drinking establishment. It actually took four people to eject him from the premises, two bar staff along with two members of the public, isn't that right, Mr Davison?"

His eyes narrowed, and his gaze bore through Sara's soul. "No comment."

"May I ask what you were hoping to achieve during the evening, Mr Davison? By hounding Bonnie Rogers?"

"I didn't. I was sitting on my bar stool when she came into the pub. I didn't move from that spot all the time she was there with her mates."

"Again, we have video footage from the incident that proves you were intimidating Miss Rogers."

"Intimidating, my arse. Is it against the law these days to watch someone with interest?"

"'Watch with interest' can also be classed as intimidation, however, we'll leave that up to the jury to decide, when, not if, the case goes to court."

"Are you frigging insane? I've done fuck all wrong except look at the bitch," he countered angrily.

"I sense there's more to this line of questioning, Inspector. Care to share where this is leading?" Ms Tyler asked, her pen poised, ready for action.

"I'll come to that in a moment, Ms Tyler. Okay, let's discuss what happened when you left, or should I say, were thrown out of the Red Admiral. Where did you go?"

"Home. Why? Has someone told you otherwise? I sense I'm being frigging stitched up here." He turned to his solicitor and said, "Ask her, find out what she's bloody getting at."

"Inspector, are you going to enlighten us about where this line of questioning is leading?"

"In good time, Ms Tyler. Mr Davison, did you go straight home on Tuesday evening? Or did you make a stop on the way? If so, where?"

"Straight home. My place is within staggering distance of the city centre, but you'll know that fact already, won't you?"

It was Sara's turn to grin. "We do indeed. What time did you arrive home on Tuesday evening?"

"Hang on a sec, I stopped off to pick up a bag of chips from the chippy at the end of my road, which meant I got home at between ten-forty-five and eleven, why?"

"That's helpful. Did you see anyone you knew on the way who can corroborate your story?"

"No, you can ask at the chippy if you don't believe me. I'm a regular in there, and Ken's an old mate of mine."

"We'll be sure to do that. What about your neighbours, did anyone see you arrive home?"

"How the fuck should I know? The old biddy next door to me was probably nosing out of her front window, like usual, but I can't say I noticed, or maybe I did at the time and I've forgotten. What the fuck is all this about? Did something happen to Bonnie?"

Sara inclined her head to the other side. "What makes you ask that particular question?"

"Doh, because of what you've just asked me, you dozy bitch."

"Mr Davison, that language is unnecessary," Tyler interjected before Sara had the chance to slap him down. "I'm advising you to curb your language when speaking to the officer."

"Whatever. I want to know what the hell is going on here, why she's asking me all these questions. I repeat, did something happen to Bonnie or one of her friends that night, and that's why you're coming after me? I have a right to know, tell me."

Sara's eyes shifted from Davison to Ms Tyler, whose eyebrows rose into her hairline.

"Yes, do tell, Inspector," Tyler insisted.

"This morning, the local pathologist requested my attendance at a crime scene." Sara allowed the words to sink in for a moment or two, then added, "When my partner and I arrived, we found the body of a young woman who has since been identified as Bonnie Rogers."

Davison slammed his fist on the table and jumped out of his seat. "What the fuck?"

The uniformed officer standing at the back of the room was the first to react. He twisted Davison's arm up his back and looked at Sara for guidance on what to do next. "Calm down, mate."

"I ain't your mate, and don't tell me to frigging calm the hell down. I can see what's going on here, and you ain't fitting me up for this. I didn't touch her, I swear I didn't."

"There's no necessity to treat my client like this, Inspector," Tyler said, aghast.

"Isn't there? My partner is in bloody hospital because of

Mr Davison's actions today. I'm afraid I've seen with my own eyes just how dangerous this man can be."

"What the fuck? It was an accident, I'm telling you, a fucking accident. But you ain't pinning what happened to Bonnie on me. This is the first I'm bloody hearing about her death. You have to believe me," he yelled, sounding desperate.

"Take him to a cell. Barry, you go with him. I think the constable is going to need a hand. And when you're ready to speak with me, Mr Davison, let the desk sergeant know, and he'll come and get me."

"Why would I want to speak to you again, bitch? I've told you, I had nothing to do with this. You're stitching me up for a crime just because it suits you, letting her real killer go free. Ha, some fucking copper you are. Get a life, open your eyes and take my word for it, I didn't do this," he shouted.

Davison tried to twist out of the grasp of the two officers, but they had no intention of releasing their grip and marched him out of the room.

Sara flopped into her chair and stared at the shocked woman sitting opposite her. She said the verbiage needed to end the interview.

"Do you honestly believe her murder is down to him?" Tyler asked.

"Yes, except I've got little to no evidence to back up that claim and if I don't find some soon… I'm going to be forced to set the bugger free, well, on that charge, although I'll throw the book at him for the attempted murder of an officer."

"That was an unfortunate consequence of his actions, however, on the flip side, maybe there's more to this than meets the eye. You have to ask yourself, would he have taken off like that if he was guilty?"

Sara sat upright. "What kind of question is that? I'm telling you this, every damn arrest I've ever made has resulted in the culprit trying to abscond, leave the scene or even the county, so forgive me for thinking your logic is way off the mark, won't you?"

"Sorry, that came out wrong." Tyler sighed. "It's just that my gut is telling me that he's innocent, and if you haven't got any evidence to back up your claim that he's killed his ex, then surely, you're up shit creek."

"Thanks for your insight. Then it's up to me and my team to find the evidence to keep that bastard sitting behind bars where he belongs. I spoke to a former girlfriend of his earlier and, let me tell you, she pretty much said the same thing. That the guy is a fucking menace to women and society as a whole. Men like him shouldn't be allowed to roam free, or don't you agree with me?"

"Of course I do, but we can't go around arresting people just because they've screwed up in life before. You need to have a word with CPS, see where you stand, Inspector, because from where I'm sitting, I'd say you were on very shaky ground with regard to him murdering his ex. All right, the attempted murder charge is a different story entirely, because as you say, you and your stand-in partner witnessed the crime and you've also got CCTV footage to back up your claim. Regarding his ex, you're going to need to get the evidence to make that one stick, and as far as I can tell, it's not likely to happen anytime soon."

"Thanks, you're not saying anything that I haven't considered myself. I'll get his alibis checked out as well and dig for the evidence we need to keep him locked up."

"I'd also like to reiterate what Davison said, if I may? About letting the real killer go free while he's sitting behind bars. Have you thought about that?"

"Of course I have. My judgement is what it should be on this case, there's no reason for you to doubt it."

Tyler cocked an eyebrow. "Even with your partner's life hanging by a thread?"

"Yes, I will not allow it to cloud my decision-making, I assure you. I'll show you out, thanks for coming."

They both stood. Sara showed the solicitor back to the reception area and shook her hand.

"Just keep digging for the evidence, I'd hate for the CPS to put the brakes on your investigation," Tyler said.

"Don't worry, we'll keep going until we find what we need to put the final nail in his coffin."

Sara trudged upstairs to find DCI Price waiting for her in her office. "Oh, shit! Sorry, ma'am, I was about to come and see you. Forgive me for not bringing you up to date sooner, it was imperative that we tracked down and arrested the suspect who we felt was trying to escape the area."

"Sod all of that, how's Carla? I'm sorry she got hurt, and why aren't you with her at the hospital?"

"Des is over there. I didn't see any point in two of us hanging around. She's in a bad way. I think that goes with the territory when a person gets flipped over a car travelling at speed."

"Fuck, poor Carla. You must have some idea of what her injuries are."

Sara shrugged. "Not really, it's hard to tell. Her heart stopped at the scene. The paramedics had to use CPR on her before they whisked her off to hospital. I'm trying to keep busy so I don't dwell on it—if I do that, I might never pick myself up again."

"I totally understand your way of thinking, Sara. If there is anything I can do, just shout. Word has it you've got the suspect downstairs, in a cell."

"That's true. We've got him for what he did to Carla but we're struggling to find any evidence to pin his ex's murder on him, but we'll keep going."

"Do you need extra manpower?"

"No, I think they'll only get in the way at this point. Can I get back to you in the event I change my mind?"

"Come here." DCI Price surprised her by holding out her arms.

Sara automatically walked into them without hesitation.

"She'll pull through," DCI Price said, "we both know she's a fighter."

Sara held back the tears pricking her eyes. "I bloody hope so. It was horrendous witnessing the accident, if you can call it that, and then dealing with the after-effects."

Price gripped Sara's arms and pushed her away slightly. "You're going to have to rid yourself of that image, Sara. Get over it in order to proceed. If you need to bend my ear about anything, just do it. Okay?"

Sara gulped and nodded. "I will, I promise. I need to get back to it. If I don't, then that's when all of this is going to hit me."

"I won't hold you up any longer. I just wanted you to know that I'm thinking about you, and Carla, of course. When will you hear?"

"When Des sees fit to call me. The last thing I want to do is start hounding him for answers."

"It's a tough call to make. If you need me to place the call, give me a shout. I'll be more than happy to lend a hand in that respect."

"Maybe we should leave it a couple of hours, allow Carla to get processed by the A and E team. I'm sure Des will contact us as soon as he hears anything, either way."

"I'll hold you all in my thoughts."

"Thanks, boss."

She watched DCI Price leave her office and cross the incident room, patting each of the team members on the shoulder as she passed their desks, which brought fresh tears to Sara's eyes. *Damn, get a grip!* Sara shook out her arms, released a couple of breaths and rejoined her team. "Right, where are we, folks?"

Craig turned to face her. "I think I might have something on one of the vans, boss."

Sara approached him. "And that is?"

"It's got false plates. Actually, they've been cloned, the real plates belong to a Mini."

"Interesting. Can you make out the driver on the footage, or am I asking too much?"

"Maybe we can catch a brief glimpse." He brought up an image that was dodgy at best, out of focus and, in Sara's opinion, was a total waste of space. "It's not good, but what it does show is that there are two people in the van."

"People? Can you be more specific?"

"If I had to take a punt, I would say there were two men."

"That's more like it, Craig. Can you track the van through the other ANPRs? Let's focus all our efforts. There's a reason it has dodgy plates. Let's run with that for now, only because we're struggling and have very little else to go on."

"Leave it with me."

Sara moved around the room to Barry's desk. "How are you holding up?"

"Don't worry about me, boss. More to the point, how are you doing?"

"I'll survive."

"I've been busy since we held the interview with Davison."

Sara's interest piqued. "I'm listening."

"I rang the chippy and spoke to Ken. He confirmed that Davison dropped in for a bag of chips and a can of Coke on Tuesday evening."

"I'm intrigued to know how he can remember what night it was."

"He said they discussed the England game which had occurred over the weekend."

"That still doesn't tell us that it was Tuesday night, does it?"

"No, you're right. Although, he also mentioned that his daughter had an aerobics session at the gym and he was having to shut up early to pick her up and take her home as his wife wasn't feeling too good."

"That's better, you're not likely to forget that sort of thing, are you?"

"That's true. I also contacted the dentist, and yes, he was telling the truth about being late for his appointment. He failed to show up."

"Hmm... it hurts that his alibis check out because I truly wanted to go ten rounds with him in the interview room."

"What now, regarding Davison?"

"I'm getting a pain in the arse, sitting on the fence with him. The couple of questions pricking my mind are, why the heck did he feel the need to run? And why did he deliberately drive at Carla?" Sara's mobile rang in her office, and she flew across the room to answer it. "DI Sara Ramsey, how can I help?"

"Sara, it's Des."

"Des, thank God, how is she? Any news yet?"

He fell silent, and her heart stopped beating for a second or two.

"Speak to me. What's going on?"

"She's going to be all right."

Relieved, Sara perched on her desk and glanced out of the window at her favourite view. "Thank God for that. Was there a doubt she wasn't going to pull through?"

"Yes, for a moment there. She's got some internal bleeding they need to tend to and a busted pelvis, so I'd say she's going to be off work for at least four to six months."

"I don't care, all I need to know is that she's still with us. Is she awake?"

"She woke up, told me she loved me and drifted off to sleep again. They're sending her up to the theatre soon."

"Thanks for letting me know, Des. How are you?"

"I'm fine. As relieved as you are by the sounds of it. Not sure what I would have done if I'd lost her. Not that she's completely out of the woods yet, but she's a few steps closer."

"Hey, I hear you. Hang in there. Will you stay with her? Do you need me to pick up any of her things from home?"

"No, I'll wait until she goes for her surgery and then take a break for a few hours. They said the operation is likely to last five to six hours. I can't hang around here all that time, it'll do my head in."

"I agree. Get out of there and freshen yourself up. Tell her I'm thinking of her and that I love her, if she wakes up again."

"I will. I'll be in touch soon, Sara."

She hung up, and the tears that had been threatening to fall for the past few hours finally cascaded down her flushed cheeks.

"Oh God, no, she hasn't, has she?" Barry asked from the doorway.

"No, don't worry, these are tears of relief. It was Des, she's going for surgery. The main thing is she's going to make it."

"Thank fuck for that."

"I'll second that. Did you want me?"

"Not really. I was being inquisitive, or nosey, whichever suits you."

"Can you tell the others? I'm going to give DCI Price a call."

Barry smiled and closed the door behind him.

Sara took a moment to get her emotions under control before she rang Carol Price. "Hi, boss, it's me. Carla is out of immediate danger. She's due to have surgery soon for a busted pelvis, and they believe some internal bleeding is going on that they're keen to tackle at the same time."

"That is good news. Ouch on the pelvis, that won't be an easy injury to come back from. Let's hope she makes a full recovery. Now, stop worrying about her and let the professionals do their job."

"In other words, get on with the task in hand, the investigation."

"Exactly. Is it your weekend off?"

"Yes, the team have all got plans. Is that a problem?"

"No, not for me. Could one person stick with the investigation, rather than let things go cold over the weekend?"

"I'll see if I can twist someone's arm to slot in a couple of hours, how's that? They're entitled to their time off just like everyone else at the station."

"Hey, I understand that. Forget I said anything."

"It's too late for that now, the damage has been done. I've had recent time off, so I might even put in a couple of hours if I can't get anyone else to cover it."

"That's not what I was saying, Sara, you need your downtime as much as anyone else."

"Yeah, but this team is my responsibility, and I never ask them to do something that I'm not prepared to do myself."

"You're a stubborn cow at times."

"I'm not about to deny it. I also understand the need to catch this murderer."

"And what about the suspect you've picked up already?"

"As much as it grieves me to say it, I'm not a hundred percent confident he's the killer."

"But you intend flinging the book at him where Carla's concerned, right?"

"Absolutely. He's not going anywhere just yet. Yes, that settles it, I'll put in a few hours over the weekend, it'll give me a chance to question him again."

"Be careful, don't burn yourself out, and you know how I feel about interviewing suspects on your own."

"Don't worry, I'll grab a couple of uniformed officers if I need to."

"We'll have a conflab on Monday, first thing, okay?"

"You've got it, boss. Have a good weekend." Sara ended the call and considered what lay ahead of her over the weekend. She glanced at her watch; it was almost five-thirty. *Bloody hell, where has the day gone?*

CHAPTER 6

"Well, that last kill was a bit of an anticlimax. I need more action and fast," Micky said. He snorted some more cocaine and leaned back as the high he'd been craving took over.

"Yeah, I don't think it was anyone's fault, not really. She was too feisty, and we wanted rid of her quickly, that's what it amounted to. Hey, go easy on that stuff, we need our wits about us if we're going to tackle another fucker tonight."

"Okay, we can't get out there for a few hours, so let's take the time to chill. You need to be more mellow, man, you're too wound up."

"Fuck off, I'm as mellow as they come. I'll get a pad and write out the note that we'll leave with the body. I love the idea of winding the police up."

"Don't forget to disguise your handwriting so it doesn't come back and bite you in the arse," Micky replied, taking yet another snort.

Saul came back with the pad and tutted. "Fuck, man, be told, will ya? Give it a rest or you'll be fit for nothing later. There's a time and a place for that shit, and this ain't it."

"Says you. Don't worry about me, I'll be there when I'm needed."

"Which is in an hour or so. We're going to need to get on the road soon. I've got an itch that needs to be scratched, so to speak."

They both laughed, Micky more exuberantly than Saul because of the dope.

"Yeah, I'm with you on that one. How are we going to do it this time?"

Saul picked up the hunting knife beside his chair and ran his finger down the jagged blade. "I think we should see what this baby can do. Maybe carve a message into the victim's torso instead of leaving a note."

Micky sat upright, his eyes widening with excitement. "I like the sound of that. Male or female?"

"Male. I prefer the competition, they always put up a fight. Women don't cut it for me, they're only good for one thing... well, maybe two at a push, cooking and screwing, or sucking my cock."

"That's three, I always thought you were crap at maths."

"I can't be good at everything, mate. Right, let's get this shit organised then. Write the note then set off. I'm going to check the van, make sure there's enough diesel in it. I ain't filled up for a few days."

"Go on then. I'll work out the details of the kill and sharpen the blade, it's trickier to do with this one."

"I wouldn't bother, you ain't had it that long."

A FEW HOURS LATER, with a full tank of diesel, they hopped in the van and drove into the heart of Hereford. Micky's gut was giving him some gyp, but he was determined not to say anything, not after Saul had warned him about snorting that crap. *Get over it. Toughen up, you wimp!*

"Which direction are we going to head in? It's dark enough that we're not likely to get seen until the last minute."

"Take a right here."

Micky did as instructed, speeding around the corner. Soon, the police station came up on their right. They stuck two fingers up as they drove past.

"Fucking tossers, the lot of them," Micky said. "They ain't got a scooby who we are or what we're up to."

"Too right. Hey, let's keep it that way, no screw-ups, right!"

"You don't need to drum it into me. We've got this sussed. Everything has gone our way so far, well, apart from the girl. That was a mishap, dumping her in the river like that."

"No more cock-ups or we'll alert the cops and have them on our tails in no time."

"I know, there's a bunch of car parks round the back of these offices, wanna take a chance? They should be near kicking out time by now."

"Why not? I reckon most of the staff will have left, what with it being a Friday night," Saul chipped in.

Micky was right. His surveillance from another job had proved invaluable for this one. "I'm gonna pull up here. Out of the way of the camera." He pointed at the security camera covering the car park from the back of the property that stopped short of reaching the spaces at the rear, where they had parked. Micky considered himself an expert on security cameras and their shortfalls.

He switched off the engine, and they waited for the handle on the back door to drop down, then they'd make their move. There was only one car left. It was a top-of-the-range Mercedes that Micky had been checking out for some time in the auto mags, hoping that one day he'd be able to afford one of his own.

"Are you sure we're in the right spot?" Saul asked. "What

if the owner has dumped his car here until later and gone off for a swift pint somewhere before he heads home?"

"Chill, relax, man." Micky watched the lights go off inside the building and made his move. "Someone's coming."

"How can you tell?"

Micky rolled his eyes. "Trust me. Let's get moving."

He led the way across the car park, and they crouched beside the door. The bar dropped, and the door swung open. Before the man noticed they were there, Micky and Saul pounced on him and knocked him to the ground.

"Get the tape and slap it over his mouth," Micky ordered.

Saul jumped into action. Micky secured the man's hands with a piece of rope, and they hoisted him to his feet. He moaned, giving the impression he was confused.

"Let's put him in the back of the van and get out of here."

"What about the camera?"

"We should have dealt with it beforehand. Let me grab a can out of the van and put it out of action."

They steered the man to the side door. Micky peered over his shoulders, ensuring the coast was still clear. It was. They'd struck lucky, and Micky giggled. The night was still young. He searched for the can of spray paint and returned to vandalise the camera whilst hiding his face.

That should do, it'll piss the cops off for sure.

He laughed and returned to the van and hopped into the driver's seat. Once Saul had secured the man's hands to the railing in the back of the van, Micky drew away and drove towards the house they had been using to keep the others.

Muffled cries came from the back, no doubt the man questioning what was going on or about to happen to him.

The excessive noise ticked Micky off. "Shut the noisy fucker up, or we'll stop over the bridge and dump him in the river."

Saul laughed. "Not again. Oi, you! Put a sock in it or my

mate here will end your life tonight, got that?"

The van fell silent, apart from the breeze whistling past Micky's head, coming from the inch-gap in the driver's window. "That did the trick. If only they were all as compliant as him, eh?"

"Yeah, if only."

Micky parked the van in the lane behind the house. They'd get the man inside, through the back door, and then he'd transfer the vehicle round the front. He left Saul to complete the task of securing their guest in the torture room, his mind already going over the pain and torment they were about to dish out on their unsuspecting victim. He enjoyed this part the most, the anticipation of what lay ahead. The surprises in store for their prisoner.

He checked the coast was clear again, more out of habit than actual need, and entered the house. The room Saul had taken the man to was soundproof, so anything they did in there wouldn't be heard by their neighbours on either side. That was the first job they'd carried out together once they'd thought up this game of theirs. That's what it was, after all. What else could it be? It had been Micky's idea initially, to kidnap total strangers on a whim, keep them for a couple of days, enough to wind up the cops. In that time, their victims would be terrorised and tortured to within an inch of their lives and brought back from the brink several times in the process, just for the fun of it. It was all about the game.

They were as twisted as each other, always had been, and Micky couldn't see that changing anytime soon. Walking into the kitchen, he removed a couple of cans of beer from the fridge and took them upstairs. Saul had tied the man to the cast-iron bedstead and was pacing the floor, his anxiety evident in his frown.

Micky threw a beer at him. Saul pulled the tab open. They chinked the cans together.

"What's wrong with your face?" Saul asked.

"Nothing. Not sure why, but I'm feeling extra anxious tonight."

"Get over it. We've got work to do before we crash for the evening. I told you to lay off the coke, didn't I?"

"Screw you, this has nothing to do with what I put in my body earlier."

"What's all this about then? Come on, let's hear it."

"Fucked if I know. My guts are playing me up something chronic."

"Go to the bloody loo and be done with it then."

"It's got nothing to do with wanting to go for a shit, why won't you be told?"

Saul shook his head. "This is the first I'm hearing about it. What's it got to do with then?"

"If I knew that, I'd do what I could to remedy the situation, tosser."

They downed the rest of the contents of the cans and threw them in the bin in the corner.

Micky wiped the remnants of the drink around his mouth on the sleeve of his jumper. "Right, where are we going to begin with this one?"

The man kicked out with his legs and twisted his body to the left and then the right, sensing and even objecting to what they might have in store for him.

Micky stepped closer to the bed and dug his elbow in the man's stomach. "Shut the fuck up. You're going to need to hold on to your strength, I'm just warning you."

Micky and Saul laughed.

"Yeah, what he said, shut the fuck up, man, and maybe we'll go easy on you," Saul whispered in the man's ear.

"Or maybe we won't," Micky added, his tone far more sinister now that the idea of what he wanted to do to their prisoner were flowing thick and fast.

CHAPTER 7

Sara didn't feel rested at all by the time Monday morning came around. She drove into work, resembling a character from *The Walking Dead*. Between her putting in a couple of hours each day at the station and finally being allowed to visit Carla in hospital, the weekend had zoomed past in a blur. Mark's had consisted of pretty much the same. He had two emergency operations to perform, one on an old cat and the other on a spaniel puppy of six months who had been overenthusiastic about chewing on a stick and had ended up with shards of splinters in his gut that Mark needed to get out before they passed naturally through the pup's system.

She had spent the morning dealing with the paperwork and emails that had escaped her attention over the weekend. A few hours into the onerous task, she glanced up to find Barry standing in the doorway. "Hi, you seem worried about something, what's wrong?"

"We've just had a call about a gruesome crime scene, boss."

"How gruesome?" she asked, unsure if her stomach could take anything too bad at that time of the morning.

"Pretty bad."

"Where?"

"Up the road from here, it's not far. You might even consider walking it, boss, it's that close."

"Really? At a residential or commercial property?"

"Commercial. Zamora's Architects."

"Should that mean something to me? If so, it doesn't, not that it matters. Okay, well, I'm not really one for walking, so we'll take my car. We're bound to be needed elsewhere afterwards, if only to break the news to the unfortunate family."

"Gotcha, yep, that thought clearly didn't cross my mind."

"I'll be with you in a few seconds. One more email to answer, and that's me done for the day."

He gave her the thumbs-up and left the room.

Sara fired off a brief answer to a very inane question from one of the departments at head office, hoping it would be a sufficient response for the survey they were conducting. As if she didn't have enough paperwork to contend with already, without having to deal with that sort of shit on a daily basis.

"Are you ready, Barry?"

"Willing and able, boss. I've got the address."

"Does the victim have a name?"

"He's the owner of the business, Jarvis Zamora."

"Damn. Okay. Let's go see what all the fuss is about. Glad my hubby didn't get the chance to treat me to a fry-up this morning, it might've had disturbing consequences."

"I stopped off for a greasy bacon sarnie on the way in. I should be able to hang on to it, at a push."

. . .

155

AT THE LOCATION, Lorraine greeted them with a concerned expression and a slightly off-hand manner.

After throwing on their protective clothing, Sara and Barry joined the pathologist and her team in the car park at the rear of the property. Sara automatically scanned the area and spotted the camera above the door. She removed her phone from her pocket and opened up the camera, zooming in. She could see the security camera had been tampered with, something she couldn't quite make out with her naked eye.

"Not good," she mumbled.

"You could say that," Lorraine said. She stared at the bloody corpse lying at her feet and shook her head.

"Sorry, just to be clear, I was talking about the state of the camera at the back door of the property."

"Ah, you noticed," Lorraine replied. "No doubt a deliberate act carried out by the killer."

"Before or after the murder?" Barry asked.

"I would hazard a guess there'd be no point in doing it after the event, so definitely before. What have we got, Lorraine, apart from the obvious?" Sara asked.

"At first glance it would appear that he was killed in situ. However, upon further examination, I can confirm the body was killed elsewhere and dumped here."

"I'm surmising you've come to that conclusion because of the amount of blood found surrounding him."

"Correct."

Sara contemplated the scenario for a moment or two, her gaze flitting between the victim and the defaced camera around ten feet away.

"I know what's running through your mind: why deface the camera if the deed was done elsewhere?"

"Yep, it doesn't make sense, not to me," Sara confirmed. "It's going to be interesting viewing the footage. Make a note to ask the staff for it once we get around to interviewing them, Barry."

"Noted, boss."

Lorraine squatted into the cramped space beside the corpse. "Do you want to join me?" she asked Sara.

Reluctantly, sensing she was about to be confronted by something bad, Sara crouched, her leg resting against the pathologist's. "Couldn't you have moved the commercial bins?"

"No doubt I could have but I didn't want to shift anything until all the photos had been taken. Stop whingeing."

"I wasn't aware that I was. What am I looking at here?"

Lorraine opened the man's shirt, and Sara almost lost her balance once she saw what was on the man's chest.

"Jesus Christ... what's that?"

"I'd say the killer carved his fate into his chest."

"What? Are you suggesting this is like the first murder? Where the note was found in his mouth?"

"Except in this poor gentleman's case, the note has been carved into his flesh."

"Oh God, that's disgusting," Barry said from behind them.

"Barry took the words out of my mouth," Sara said. "What the fuck are we dealing with here?"

Lorraine tutted. "Apart from a very warped killer, I'm not sure if I can give a definitive answer to that. Give me time, and I'll hopefully come up with the goods."

"You haven't let me down yet."

"I know we should be dealing with the case, but I have to ask, what with you not mentioning it or giving me a call to update me over the weekend, how's Carla doing?"

"She's still in a lot of pain. The surgery was a success in that they stopped the internal bleeding and put a metal plate in her pelvis."

Lorraine cringed. "I hope she's keeping her spirits up. That type of injury could take months to heal."

"Yeah, I'm not an expert, but I thought the same. Poor Carla, I know she was complaining she needed a rest, but I don't think she was bargaining on something like this and taking an enforced one. Back to business… What else have we got? Any suggestions why the body was dumped here? Apart from it being his place of business… aww… no, forget I said that. It's probably the killer making a point, playing mind games with either the victim's colleagues or the police and you lot."

"More than likely the latter," Lorraine agreed.

"Who found him?" Sara asked.

"A member of staff. She was putting the rubbish in the bin and saw his leg poking out at the side. I told her you'd be wanting a word with her soon; she was all for taking off, going home because of the shock."

"Thanks, then we'd better go and see her. Anything else for us, Lorraine?"

"I'll give you a shout if I stumble across anything else. We'll be shifting him to the mortuary once all the photographs and evidence have been dealt with. I need to get him out of this weather. Rain is forecast to hit us in an hour or so."

"We'll get out of your hair and start interviewing the staff inside. Thanks, Lorraine. Get the report back to me ASAP, if you would?"

"Don't I always?"

"Debatable at times."

Lorraine glowered, and Sara knew when to back away before her friend let loose with a barrage of insults.

"Speak later."

"You can count on it, young lady," Lorraine called after her.

Barry sniggered while they removed their protective clothing and placed it in the awaiting black bag.

"You can pack that in," Sara reprimanded him. She laughed at his expression; it was obvious he was unsure whether she was joking or not. "I'm teasing you. You'll get used to all the banter out in the field, it's what brightens our moods most days."

"I bet. It's definitely a learning curve. I'm enjoying being with you. Thanks for asking me to fill in for Carla. I hope I don't let you down."

"I have a feeling you'll slot in nicely, and you've never let me down in the past, so why should you being at my beck and call on this investigation be any different? Chip in with a question here and there if you believe I've missed anything, within reason, of course."

"Oh yes, I wouldn't dream of stepping on your toes, boss. Maybe I'll leave my observations until we've left the scene or completed an interview, how's that?"

"Surely it'll be too late by then. Speak up when you can, I promise I won't be offended—if the question has merit, of course."

"I'll do my best."

They left the car park and rounded the building to enter the front door of the property. Three women, with mugs in their hands, stood in the reception area, giving Sara the impression that they were shell-shocked.

Sara flashed her ID and introduced herself and Barry. "Can I ask who found the body?"

The older of the three women put a hand in the air. "I did. Although I wish I hadn't. Bloody shaken me up terrible, it has. Poor Mr Zamora."

"I'm going to need to question all of you. Is there anywhere private we can hold the interviews?"

"I suppose we could do it in his office, or would that be too insensitive?" the same woman asked.

Sara shrugged. "Suits me, if it's fine with you ladies."

They all nodded. The older woman suggested they follow her up the narrow hallway to a large office at the rear, over-looking the car park, where Zamora's body had been found.

"I can't stop thinking about it, finding him out there like that. I didn't know what to do about telling his wife. She's usually around but has been away at a business conference over the weekend, and I don't know if she's back yet or not."

"Don't worry, we should be the ones to break the news."

"Phew! I'm glad I don't have to deal with it. Katia is going to be devastated, we all are. Who could do such a callous thing? Mr Zamora was such a kind and thoughtful man. I've never known him to have an argument with anyone, not in the office. He was always extremely fair with the staff, gave us time off if we needed it, that sort of thing. Nothing was too much effort, and he was constantly putting his staff first. Ran this place like clockwork, and because of his fairness, the staff never took the piss and only asked for time off if it was truly needed. I know I'll never work for a better boss."

"He sounds a remarkable man. He was an architect, yes?"

"Yes, both he and his wife are. She deals mainly with the public, and Jarvis predominantly worked with the local busi-nesses on the commercial side. They had everything covered that way, rarely crossed into each other's territories. Although, I suppose they did on occasion, but not very often."

"And as far as you know, there's never been any aggro from a client? Perhaps in recent weeks or months?"

"I'm shocked that you should ask that. No, never. Jarvis had a mantra: 'The client is God and always right'. He lived and breathed by that saying. Bent over backwards to ensure that clients were always treated with utmost respect. Keen to bring their ideas to fruition and point them in the right direction if there were any lingering doubts about a design."

"I see, and what about his wife?"

"Pretty much the same."

"Sorry, I didn't catch your name?"

"I'm the one who should apologise. How remiss of me not to tell you until now. It's Jerry, Geraldine; I hate it and prefer to be called Jerry."

"I love Geraldine. Perhaps you can tell me about their marriage. Did they have any children?"

"No, they were trying to have them but they were struggling. They deserved to put the cherry on the top of the cake. They had everything else, only children were missing from their lives. They worked non-stop to get this place up and running, put off having children for a few years, but he let it slip a few months ago that they were in the process of going down the fertility route and hoping to have good news soon. I feel sorry for Katia, she has always been desperate to have children, and now… their dream will never be fulfilled."

"Very sad indeed. So you would class the couple as happily married?"

"Absolutely. They had one of the best marriages going. In the past six months, once the business was truly established, they took time off together, regularly, went on different adventures, either at the weekend or sometimes even during the week if there was a lull in the business."

"I have to ask this question, forgive me if you find it offensive. Could either one of them have been having an affair?"

"I can categorically tell you that the answer is no. They were like teenagers around the office. Touching each other discreetly when they thought no one was watching. I would have called it a Mills and Boon type romance, not the *Fifty Shades* kind. She blushed a lot every time he spoke to her. It was adorable. I believe a lot of couples would have been envious of what they had."

Sara wondered if Jerry had realised what she'd said but decided not to challenge her about her choice of words.

"Who generally locked up around here?"

"Mr Zamora. We usually leave earlier on a Friday. A few of us go for a drink after work at the local down the road."

"So would that have been the last time you saw your boss?"

"Yes, Friday evening. We all left just after five. He said he had a few plans to print off before he could call it a day, and Katia drove north around two that afternoon, so he didn't mind staying later than usual and insisted we get off early."

"Did he work over the weekend at all?"

"No, he had no intention of coming in, told me he was intending to go fishing with a few of his mates while Katia was away enjoying herself at the conference. I believe he was being sarcastic with that comment." She shook her head and wiped away a tear. "He had a wicked sense of humour at times. People loved being in the same room as him, and now he's gone. I still can't take it in, how someone could have gone to such extremes as to kill him."

"Well, we're here to figure that out. I have to ask about the camera overlooking the car park. How long has it been out of action?"

"Excuse me? I didn't realise it was. Jarvis was super keen to have this place secure and installed the camera a few years ago, when we started getting super busy."

"Do you have access to the footage from it? Or was that his department?"

"Hazel is your girl for anything technical like that, you'd be better off speaking to her rather than me."

"Can we do that now? It's important we view the footage in case it can give us a clue about the murderer."

Jerry pushed back her former boss' executive chair and ran from the room. She returned a few moments later with one of the other ladies, who had slipped on a pair of spectacles since Sara had last seen her.

"This is Hazel, she's an absolute genius with everything to do with the computers and cameras around here."

Sara smiled at the brunette. "Hi, Hazel. I wondered if you might be able to help us out. Did you notice if the camera was working last week?"

"Yes, it was. I'm the one in charge of changing the discs every day. Not that it crossed my mind to do it this morning... what with what's going on out there."

"I understand. It's been defaced. Is there any chance you can view the footage from Friday for us? Check around the time that you guys left, see if Jarvis had a visitor before he left for the evening."

"I'll get on it right away. Will you give me five minutes?"

"Take your time."

Hazel left the room, and Jerry returned to her seat once more.

"I bet she'll have something for you shortly. It's amazing what she can do with all that stuff. Are you sure you wouldn't like a tea or coffee while you wait?"

"We're fine, but thanks for the offer. How many staff are there?"

"Just the three of us, plus Jarvis and Katia." Jerry gasped. "She needs to know, to be told about him."

"When was she due back from her weekend away?"

"Late last night. I would have thought she'd have been here by now. Oh God, you don't think anything has happened to her, as well? What if it was some kind of plan to rob the place? Bump him off, go to the house, only to find Katia missing... oh, I don't know, I'm probably talking bloody nonsense as usual, trying my best to be Poirot, to solve the complex crime."

"It's natural for your imagination to run riot at a time like this."

Hazel reappeared in the doorway. "I found something you should see."

Sara and Barry tore down the corridor after her into a small room where the computer equipment was housed. On one of the larger screens was a half picture of a young man.

"Bloody hell… what an idiot!" Barry shouted.

"Nailed the bastard. Excuse my language," Sara said to Hazel who flipped her apology away with her hand.

"Do you recognise him, Barry?"

"I can't say I do. If we can get a clearer image, we'll be able to run it through the system."

Sara glanced at Hazel, who pressed a button and went back and forth over the image a few times. "What about this? It's the best I can do, I think."

"Seems perfect to me," Sara said. "What do you reckon, Barry?"

"It's better. I wouldn't say it was perfect, boss." His head whipped around, and he muttered an apology.

She dug him in the ribs. "We're all entitled to our opinion."

Suddenly, a lot of shouting could be heard from the reception area. Intrigue got the better of Sara, and she rushed out of the room to find a very slender, tall, dark-skinned woman leaning against the counter.

"This can't be true, it can't be. Not Jarvis… not my Jarvis."

"Shit! It's Katia," Jerry said from behind her.

Sara approached the distraught woman and produced her ID. "Mrs Zamora, I'm DI Sara Ramsey. I'm the Senior Investigating Officer on your husband's case."

"Why haven't I been told? Why didn't someone tell me?"

Jerry held her hand up. "I'm sorry, Katia, that's down to me, I... we... didn't know how to tell you."

"I was delayed getting home. There was a mix-up at the conference. I tried all weekend to call Jarvis and I thought he must have been out of range. He said something about going off on one of his fishing trips with his friends. Sometimes he even chooses to leave his phone at home, so I wasn't really that concerned about him."

Sara nodded. "Ah, I wondered if he had been reported missing over the weekend or not. That will save us time checking. Forgive me, I'm so sorry for your loss. Can we get you a drink?"

"No, all I want is for you to tell me what's going on around here. Why? I mean how? I don't even know how to start. What's going on?"

"Why don't we go through to his office, or yours if you have one, and I'll go over the details we have to do with the case so far."

"I share an office with my husband. No, I don't want to go anywhere else, here will do. I want the rest of my team to hear this first-hand. They have as much right to know what's gone on around here as I do. We're all very close. So, please tell us."

"Jerry arrived this morning to find your husband's body out the back, behind the bins. She called nine-nine-nine as soon as she made the discovery. I've had a word with the pathologist, and we're of the same opinion that your husband was murdered by the person who killed another man at the beginning of last week."

"What? Why haven't you caught this person?"

"In our defence, we do have a suspect in custody, but that was to do with yet another case we're working on."

Katia frowned and shook her head. She faced the three women huddled together behind her and asked, "Is any of this making any sense to you? Because I'm well and truly lost here. I haven't got a bloody clue what you've just said. All I really heard was that you have a suspect in custody. What happened? Did you leave the cell door open and allow him to escape, or what?"

"My mistake. Let me clarify my point. A suspect was arrested on Friday whom we presumed had killed his ex-girlfriend…" Sara stopped. Even her own rambling about Davison was confusing the hell out of her. She faced Barry to see if he could lend a hand.

He averted his eyes, indicating that she was on her own.

"I'm still not with you. You have two murders. Are you telling me they're connected?" Katia asked.

"Possibly. There's a very loose connection in that both victims had been abducted and were found a few days later. But we're actually investigating three murders this week." *If the three crimes are linked. For all I know, I could be talking out of my arse, which I probably am if Davison has been banged up in a cell all weekend, awaiting a trip to the remand centre.*

"Forget I said anything," Sara said, "it's been a long couple of days and…"

"I don't want to hear any excuses. All I'm bothered about is why someone came here and killed my husband. One of the nicest people I have ever had the pleasure of knowing. Why? If you can't answer a simple question like that then maybe you're in the wrong job, Inspector. Or maybe you should come back and speak to me when you have some-thing definitive to tell me. I'm lacking any confidence in your capabilities right now. Forgive me for coming down hard on you, but that's my husband lying dead out there, not yours."

"I totally understand you being narked with me. It's been a harrowing weekend as the suspect we have in custody tried to murder my partner as well. She's still in hospital now."

"I'm sorry," Katia mumbled. "But that doesn't excuse you

coming here and trying to confuse the hell out of me when all I want to hear are the facts or the truth about what's going on. Someone killed my husband: do you know who that person is or not?"

"We have an inkling. Hazel showed us an image of whom we suspect to be the killer. He was in the process of damaging the camera overlooking the car park at the rear. I can only presume it was to disguise what he was about to do to your husband. The one niggling doubt in my mind, about that scenario, is that the pathologist has informed me that she believes your husband wasn't killed here."

"I don't understand. What are you telling us?"

"That the pathologist believes that your husband was probably kidnapped, kept elsewhere, possibly over the weekend, and then his body was returned here so that he would be easily discovered."

"But that's… insane. Jarvis went away with friends, fishing," Katia replied. She removed her phone from her jacket pocket and dialled a number. "I'll check with Nikel."

"Thanks," Sara replied.

Katia put the phone on speaker. "Nikel, it's Katia. Were you with Jarvis over the weekend? Did you go fishing with him?"

"Sorry, Katia, I had to call it off at the last minute because my father was taken ill. I rang him Friday at around four. He told me that it didn't matter, he would work over the weekend instead, catch up on a few ideas he wanted to put in place around there. Why? What's wrong?"

Katia exhaled a large breath. "Bugger, I'm sorry to be the one to tell you this… Jarvis is dead, he's here at the office, in the car park, he's been murdered. The police and SOCO are all over the place. My head's a mess, I can't think straight."

"Holy shit! Do they know what happened to him? Do you want me to come over there and be with you? I'm at the hospital, fifty miles away, but I can leave here to be with you, it's no problem."

"No, let me deal with the police and get back to you later. I needed to find out if Jarvis was with you or not. Sending much love to you and your family. Keep me updated on your father's progress."

"I will. My condolences. I don't think it's sunk in yet, he was a fine man and the best of friends, to all of us. Ring me if you need me, for anything, day or night."

"Thank you. Speak soon." She ended the call and spun around to face Sara. "You heard that. What is your conclusion?"

"We've got a time when the camera was damaged. The image said it happened at five-forty-six on Friday. Hazel, can I ask you to make me a copy of the last ten minutes on the disc, please?"

"Of course. I'll sort that out for you now." She scampered off, a determined woman on a mission.

"I have to ask if either you or your husband have had any form of trouble lately, Katia. Either at work or at home, perhaps with a neighbour, an ex-partner, anything in that vein?"

Katia paused for a moment or two to consider the question. "No, nothing that is coming to mind at all. We prefer a quiet life. Have always treated people the way we expect ourselves to be treated. Our neighbours are all very kind to us, despite our heritage and colour, but then, we live in a good area, not that it should matter. I can't think of a single reason why someone would want to harm Jarvis, let alone kill him. What about the other victims, what did their families say?"

Sara shrugged. "Pretty much the same."

"What does that tell you?" Katia asked, confusion wrinkling her brow. She swept her long black hair over her shoulder and folded her arms.

"That we probably have a killer amongst us who is choosing his victims at random."

"And how are you going to find them, or more importantly, prevent them from killing someone else and destroying yet another family's life?" Katia demanded.

"Once we have the copy of the disc from Hazel, we can get to work identifying the man in the picture. If necessary, I'll go on air, ask the press officer at the station to call a conference. You should know this about me and my team, Katia: we're a determined bunch and have a superb and enviable success rate. Please, don't give up on us before we've had a chance to begin our investigation."

Hazel returned and handed Sara a disc in a plastic case.

"Thank you, this is really going to help our investigation."

"I hope it does. Is there anything else you need from us?" Katia asked.

"I don't think so. I'll leave you a couple of my cards. If any of you should think of something that you feel would help our investigation, please do get in touch with me."

"We will. Good luck. When are you likely to apprehend a suspect?" Katia enquired.

Sara sighed. "Very soon, hopefully. I don't suppose the names Adam Pearce or Bonnie Rogers mean anything to you, do they?"

"No, should they?"

"They're the other victims we're dealing with at present. If there's a link to the crimes, I wondered if it was because they knew each other."

"No, sorry. I can't help you there."

"It's not a problem. Once again, our condolences on your loss."

"Thank you." Katia turned and walked towards her office.

Sara and Barry left the building and revisited the crime scene but kept their distance, not willing to waste another protective suit.

"Lorraine, anything else for us before we leave?" Sara asked.

Lorraine left the scene and approached Sara but stopped around five feet from her. "Nothing as such. Only to tell you that I believe the wounds were made by a jagged knife."

"Like a hunting knife?" Barry asked.

Lorraine jerked her head in his direction "Exactly the knife I had in mind. The message may have been written by another blade. I don't think we'll ever find that out until we capture the culprit and they reveal all. Was that the wife who showed up?"

"Yes, very upset, as you can imagine." Sara glanced over her shoulder to check there was no chance of her being over-heard. "We've got a possible image of the suspect from the camera before it was destroyed."

"Very interesting. A clear picture?"

"Relatively. We might need to call on the lab to enhance it for us. Can I get back to you on that?"

"Of course. Did you find out anything else?"

"He was due to go fishing, but the arrangements were called off on Friday afternoon, so he was still here only by chance, it wasn't a regular occurrence. Also, something struck me in there, something I haven't had a chance to process fully."

"Go on, what's on your mind, Sara?"

"Maybe all three deaths in the past week are linked, only because the three suspects appear to have been abducted a couple of days before their bodies have shown up."

Lorraine chewed on her pink-tinged lips. "Now that's interesting, might be worth further investigation on your part."

"Yeah, maybe. Our priority at the moment is doing all we can to trace the person we suspect we've caught on camera."

"Let me know how you get on." Lorraine held out her hand. "I felt a drop of rain. I need to get the victim moved before anything comes of it."

"Makes sense to me. We'll get back to the station now we don't have the chore of chasing down and informing the next of kin," Sara said.

"Handy when they show up at a crime scene. Hush my mouth. I shouldn't joke, not at a time like this."

"I'll let you off. Speak to you soon."

"My report will be winging its way to you within the next twenty-four to thirty-six hours."

BACK AT THE STATION, Sara's first port of call was to drop in to see the station's press officer, Jane Donaldson, in person.

"Hello, you. What brings you here, or is that a dumb question?" Jane said with a knowing smile.

Sara sank into the vacant chair next to Jane's desk. "I've got a bummer of an investigation on the go—actually, three of them. All or none of which might be connected."

"You've lost me, what does that mean?" Jane picked up a biro and pulled her notebook in front of her.

"I wish I bloody knew. What it boils down to is that three victims have lost their lives this week. The key point of me seeking out your input into this complex matter is that I've just come from the final crime scene with what can only be considered as incriminating evidence."

"Ooo… sounds intriguing. Well, don't stop there."

"The CCTV camera at the victim's place of work was vandalised, and we have a pretty clear image of the man who carried out the dastardly deed and is obviously a person of interest whom I'm eager to speak with."

"Gosh, that was pretty careless of him, or was it?"

Sara puffed out her cheeks and twisted her mouth from side to side. "Hard to tell. I'm hoping against hope that he's messed up big time, but who knows what twisted fuckers like him have running through their minds or the games people of his ilk enjoy getting up to? Maybe he's one of these tossers who gets a hard-on when he toys with the police. We've had our fair share of mongrels like that in the past, haven't we?"

"You have indeed. So when do you need the conference set up for?"

"ASAP. The image should be sorted within the next twenty minutes, according to my stand-in partner."

"Is Carla on holiday?"

"Try in hospital and you'd be nearer the mark."

Jane shot forward in her chair. "What? Why? Is she having an op for a procedure? Or is she pregnant?"

"It's complicated. In a nutshell, we went to visit a suspect on Friday, and the moron mowed her down. She had internal bleeding and a fractured pelvis. Her heart stopped at the scene. I was sent into panic mode until the paramedics arrived."

"Damn, I hadn't heard. Poor Carla. She's going to be all right though, isn't she? She'll pull through and come back to work?"

"Christ, I hope so. There's no doubt in my mind, or there wasn't, until you raised the subject."

Jane slapped a hand over her mouth, and Sara laughed.

"Maybe we should move on."

Jane dropped her hand again and nodded. "It might be a wise thing to do. Let me make some calls and get back to you in what? Ten minutes? Yes, that should cover it."

"I knew I could rely on you. I'll be in the incident room. Contact me via my mobile or my landline in my office. I'll be bringing the rest of the team up to date on the latest victim."

"And don't forget to chase up the image. If you can present that at the conference, the journalists will love you forever."

"You reckon? Are you sure you're not going over the top there? As if I could forget, that picture is the main reason I've requested the conference. Let's hope someone can put a name to the culprit. Boy, could we do with a break to get this investigation on the right track? If the three cases are somehow connected, we're bloody looking at yet another serial killer being in our midst."

"Heck, I never thought about that angle. Do you know what this person's motive is for killing the victims?"

"No, nothing at all to indicate that the victims are even connected, as yet. At this stage it's pure conjecture on my part because I believe there's a possible pattern."

"And that would be?" Jane asked, her brow pinching into neat little creases.

"The three victims were all kidnapped or abducted, however you want to phrase it, before their bodies showed up a few days later."

"Very strange. Anything else?"

Sara laughed. "You can read me like a book. Yes, two of the victims had messages either on, or in them, stating by what method they were going to be killed."

"Bloody Nora. The gall of the killer, eh?"

"I know, it takes all sorts to make up this shitty world of ours."

"You're not wrong. Right, leave it with me. I'll call you when I've finalised everything."

"In other words, get out of my hair and make yourself useful elsewhere."

They both laughed, and Sara walked back to the incident

room deep in thought. The ever-efficient Barry had a surprise waiting for her in the shape of a relatively clear image. The only drawback was that the picture showed only half the killer's face.

Sara surveyed the photo and shook her head. "It's not good enough, is it?"

Barry shrugged. "We'll have to wait and see what joy we get from the conference."

"Yeah, I was hoping to be able to present something better, but this will have to do. It's definitely the best available, yes?"

He raised an eyebrow.

"Okay, it was a silly question, forget I asked. Can you run me off a couple of copies? I'm waiting to hear back from the press officer, but in the meantime, I'll run one downstairs to Jeff, get him to circulate it amongst his guys on the streets."

"Why don't I do that for you?" Barry suggested.

Sara smiled and winked at him. "What a mighty fine idea that would be. Right, this is what we're up against with this latest victim."

Barry did what he had to do at the copier and left the room while Sara went over the details of the crime they had attended. Barry returned as Sara was summing up the situation and the theory that could mean a possible link to all three crimes.

Christine spoke first. "Do you want us to see if there are any connections to all three victims?"

"Honestly, no, because I think it will be a waste of our time. I've already asked Katia Zamora if she had heard of Adam and Bonnie, and she said no. So I think we'll leave that there for now, maybe revisit it if nothing else grabs our attention."

Sara's mobile jingled in her pocket. "Hi, Jane. I'm praying you've got some good news for me."

"I have. Well, it depends on how you feel about sitting in front of a bunch of hungry journalists at midday."

"Blimey, you amaze me every time. That's fine by me. Thanks, Jane. I'll see you downstairs five minutes before."

"Any luck on enhancing the image to make it useable?"

"The jury is still out on the results for that one. I'll bring it with me. You can have the final decision as to whether we use it or not."

"That's a huge responsibility. Thanks for heaping it on my shoulders."

Sara giggled. "I haven't yet. I'll see you later." She ended the call and picked up where she had left off, going over a few details that needed her attention. Having left the team to get on with their various chores, she spent the rest of the morning in her office, making notes for the conference she would attend later. Sara then rang DCI Price, bringing her up to speed with the third victim. The DCI wasn't happy that the evidence was minimal on the case, but her spirits rose when Sara mentioned that she was about to hold a press conference and that she had a possible lead on the main suspect. As usual, the chief left everything in her capable hands and asked for an update at the end of the day.

THE JOURNALISTS BEHAVED themselves for a change, but they also agreed that the image Sara had shown them wasn't the best for them to be working with, however, they agreed to go along with it and get it out there in the public domain.

Now it was a nervous waiting game for all the pieces of the puzzle to slot into place. Craig volunteered to man the phones that evening. Sara had seen enough of the incident room over her weekend stint so was happy for him to take the lead, on the proviso that he rang her straight away if anything of note surfaced.

The staff drifted off, and she was left with Barry and Craig.

"Thanks for standing in for Carla today, Barry."

"I think we'll make a great team going forward, boss... umm... until Carla is fit to return," he added swiftly, his cheeks turning red.

"Lord knows when that is likely to be, given the injuries she's suffered. That reminds me, I need to check how Davison is bearing up at the remand centre." She grinned.

"I hope he's getting sleepless nights and a bucketload of shit thrown at him," Craig threw in.

Barry shook his head. "I think he'll be receiving slaps on the back and a lot of praise, you know, for taking down a copper on duty. We all know what warped fuckers they can be on the inside."

"Unfortunately, I think you're probably right," Sara said. "Okay, I'm calling it a day. Ring me, Craig, and don't stay any longer than ten-thirty. Oh, and don't bother coming in until twelve tomorrow."

"Thanks, boss, I'll see how it goes. You know what I'm like, always eager to get on with my day. I'd feel lost wandering around the house all morning, feeling useless."

"Yeah, I'm the same. The offer is there. See how you feel in the morning, and don't forget to ring me if anything comes to light this evening."

"I won't. Have a rest if you can. Who knows what lies ahead of us over the coming days?"

SARA AND MARK had eaten a special meal together. Sara had recently bought an Instant Pot, much to Mark's amusement. Her excuse for purchasing yet another kitchen gadget was that it would save time and money, especially when batch cooking meals at the weekend for her to shove in the freezer.

On the menu that night was a beef casserole with creamy mashed potatoes. The whole meal had taken around an hour to cook, and the results shocked both of them.

"What kind of sorcery is this?" Mark asked, suitably impressed. He flicked through the pages of the instructions.

"I'm amazed at how tender that beef was and I have to confess they were the best mashed potatoes I've ever tasted. No offence intended to the meals you cook all the time."

"Hey, who am I to argue with you? This machine is going to be a godsend. I can't wait to make a curry at the weekend. We can put the excess in the freezer for a mid-week feast. You can never have too many curries in a week, and it'll be healthier for us than a takeaway."

Sara was thrilled that Mark was as enthusiastic about the new gadget as she was, and the washing up was an absolute breeze, too, one huge pot as opposed to three or four on the stove at the same time. She was in the middle of clearing the table when her phone rang.

"I'd better get this, in case Craig has any news from the press conference that has aired this evening."

"Hey, I'm not about to stand in your way after you've just served up that fantastic meal. I'll feed Misty and nip up and get changed." He kissed her on the way past.

"Hi, Craig. How's it going?"

"I didn't think you'd mind me disturbing your evening with this news, boss."

"Sounds intriguing, go on." Sara dropped into a chair at the kitchen table and braced herself.

"The desk sergeant passed a call through to me from a witness who had seen something he thought could be related to the press release from the conference earlier today."

"I'm listening."

"He was out walking his dog and spotted something disturbing across the park from where he lives."

"Okay, and what was that?"

"He saw a couple of men approach a man at the back of his van. He witnessed the owner of the van shout at the two other men, and they lashed out at him. Knocked him out and bundled him in the back of his vehicle and drove off."

"Shit. Where was this?"

"Down by the racecourse, the park that runs alongside it, or is very close to it, I think. Sorry, I'm not really sure. I should have got a definite location from him. Shall I call him back?"

"Yes, we're going to need that, Craig. Is the witness at home?"

"Yes, he was a bit shaken up. In my defence, I didn't want to keep him on the phone for too long because of how upset he was. His wife had instructed him to call the station."

"Is it worth me calling round there to see him?"

"I can't see what harm it could do. Do you want me to come with you? It's been relatively quiet around here up until that call came in."

"Yes, meet me at his house. I'd prefer to get the interview out of the way while the details are still fresh in his mind."

Craig gave her the address and told her he'd confirm where the incident had taken place and meet her at Cyril Tetley's residence in thirty minutes.

Mark came downstairs and was surprised to find Sara putting her shoes and coat on. "Don't tell me they've called you in?"

"They haven't. Something major has cropped up, and I've volunteered to nip out and interview a witness to another possible kidnapping. Sorry, Mark, you know I wouldn't go if I didn't think it was necessary to attend." She leaned in for a kiss.

"I know. I was going to show you my appreciation for cooking me that wonderful dinner tonight."

"I shouldn't be too long, I hope. Keep those ideas for later, okay?"

"If you insist. Stay safe out there. Hey, I might even knock up the curry tonight, save me doing it at the weekend."

Sara laughed. "Sounds like a great idea to me. I bet it turns out to be amazing. Gotta fly, love you, thanks for understanding."

"Always. Love you, too."

CHAPTER 8

"We did it, we got another one. All right, it wasn't ideal bundling him into the back of his own van, but we had to take the chance while the opportunity presented itself," Micky said. He punched the air once they had put their prisoner in the torture room.

"How come, if I had suggested that, I would have been kicked into touch?" Saul complained.

"Bollocks. Now all we need to do is pick up our van and dump his."

"We can do that later, I'm starving. I'm going to nip down the chippy. What do you want?"

"Cod and chips with a battered sausage on the side."

"On your bike. Cough up. You can pay for your own if you're going the full hog."

Micky pulled a twenty from his wallet. "And get us a large bottle of lemonade while you're there, too."

"If that's enough to cover it. I'll be back soon."

With Saul out of the way, for the next half an hour, Micky got to work making notes on how the kill should happen. Never one for sitting in silence, he switched on the TV to find the local news on. He couldn't believe his eyes when he saw part of his face there on the screen.

"What the fuck?" He stood and flung his chair across the room. It broke into pieces. He kicked out at it, making it splinter into even more pieces. "Shit! How the heck am I going to get out of this one?"

Saul returned with their dinner fifteen minutes later to find Micky pacing the floor. "Everything all right? What's with the chair?"

"I had to take my frustrations out on something."

"What frustrations? You shouldn't have any. It mostly went to plan. All we've got to do is switch the vehicles over."

"Not true. We're up fucking shit creek. I've just watched the local news, and my face was plastered all over it."

Saul dropped the wrapped chippy supper on the kitchen table and stared at him. "What? How come?"

"The camera from the architect's office. Half my face was showing on the footage."

Saul frowned. "Only half of it? That should be okay then, shouldn't it?"

"No way, man. I'm telling you, if any of my enemies see that tonight, they'll be straight on the damn blower to the cops, supplying them with my name, I can guarantee it."

"Then we're screwed. What are we going to do with him upstairs?"

"We've got to get rid of him, and his bloody van, tonight. Then I think we should skip town, the county, the country even, in case they widen the search."

"Shit, what if the nationals want to pick up on the story?"

"The thought had crossed my mind. It's all conspiring against us. We've screwed up."

"Correction, *you've* screwed up," Saul snarled.

"Shit, and don't I know it? You don't have to twist the

knife in my gut, as well." He saw a spark in his mate's eyes. "You wouldn't dare?"

Saul's gaze flicked around the room, searching for something. Micky realised what was tearing through his mate's mind and ran towards the hunting knife his partner kept in the drawer on the far wall. Except Saul had the same idea and got there before him.

"Get back," Saul ordered, the blade three inches from Micky's midriff.

"Come on, man, don't do this. We'll put our thinking caps on and come up with something to get us out of this shit."

"The shit you got us in. From what I can tell, I'm pretty much in the clear and I'm determined to keep it that way."

"What happened to us being the dream team? What are you saying?"

"That I don't give a shit about playing the game any more. I preferred it when the stakes weren't so high." Saul jabbed with the knife, and it caught Micky in the side.

Micky clutched at the wound, too stunned to cry out as the blood seeped through his fingers. "Up yours. You can't do this to me. I'm the frigging brains of this operation."

"Maybe that was the mistake I made, allowing you to be in charge. Look where it has sodding well got us. We're screwed and, in my eyes, there's only one way out of it."

Micky tried to defend himself with his hands, but it was an impossible task. Saul came at him and repeatedly stabbed him until Micky sank to his knees, pain etched on his face.

"I thought we were friends."

"The games people play, mate, they never turn out the way they're expected to, ain't that right?" Saul laughed and walked out of the room.

Micky shouted after him, but the weakness impairing his body was a stumbling block. Darkness came quickly. It was a welcome relief in the end.

. . .

SARA PULLED up outside the house of the witness at the same time as Craig got there. "Hi, how far is the park from here?"

"It's to the right of us, less than two hundred yards or so."

"Okay, I like to get my bearings. Let's see what the old man can tell us."

They walked up the path of the semi-detached house with its pretty front garden on either side of them.

"Someone takes pride in their garden," she said.

"If he and his wife are retired, they'll have plenty of time on their hands," Craig replied.

"God, don't let my father hear you say that. He's been retired years and reckons he works harder now than when he was in full-time employment."

Craig rolled his eyes and rang the bell. "Something to look forward to. I was hoping life would slow down considerably by the time I reach retirement age."

"Maybe a little planning ahead will go a long way towards succeeding with that ambition."

The door opened behind her. She turned to face an elderly gentleman with a worried expression fixed in place. "Hello, Mr Tetley. I'm DI Sara Ramsey, and this is my partner, DC Craig Watson. Will it be all right if we come in and speak with you?"

"Yes, yes, come right in. Sylvia, the police are here. Stick the kettle on, will you?" he bellowed.

His wife appeared in the doorway at the end of the hallway and wagged a finger at her husband. "There's no need to shout, I'm in the kitchen not at the bottom of the ruddy garden. It's already on. Tea or coffee?"

"Coffee and sugar for both of us, thank you," Sara called back with a wave.

"Come through to the lounge. No need to take your shoes

off, we have dark carpets throughout for that very reason, so they don't show the dirt." He led the way into a dated lounge adorned with dozens of family photos on every surface. "Take a seat. Now, Jack, stop growling or I'll put you outside."

The Jack Russell, sitting in his basket by the fire, instantly quietened down but kept its beady eye on them until Sara and Craig sat on the sofa, leaving the two armchairs free.

"I'm still shaken up by what I saw. Well, you don't expect to see a real-life kidnapping, do you?"

"They're few and far between, sir, thankfully. Can you tell me at what time the incident occurred?" Sara asked.

Craig removed his notebook to jot down the details.

"I think it must have been around six-thirty. I nipped out after the local news had been on. I saw that story they were running, and that's what made me ring up and tell you, truth be told. Well, that and the wife's nagging."

Sylvia pushed open the door and deposited the tray of mugs on the coffee table. "I heard that. I wasn't nagging, I was prompting you to do the right thing. The police need to know about incidents like this, love, otherwise these awful crimes will never get solved if folks like us keep schtum, isn't that right?" she asked Sara.

"Absolutely, Mrs Tetley. Crimes of this magnitude need to be investigated as soon as they arise."

"All right, I'm glad I rang the station, now. What are you doing about that poor man?"

"An alert has been put out, but we're going to need you to furnish us with a few more details before an arrest can be made, sir."

"I was out walking Jack at the park down the road. This man came out of the house opposite, quite a distance from me. I didn't take that much notice of him, not at first. It wasn't until Jack stopped to do his business that I turned to see what was going on."

"And what was that?" Sara sipped at her drink.

"Be patient, I'm trying to put things in the order of how they happened. That's important to you people, isn't it?"

"Indeed. Sorry to interrupt, you carry on."

"This man was putting his equipment in the back of his van, and another white van pulled up a few feet in front of him. Two men got out and approached the other man. He was all smiles to begin with, but things soon turned sour between them. By this time, I was fascinated by what I was seeing but also cautious. I didn't want to get involved so kept quiet. There was a tree nearby, one with a thick trunk. I slipped behind it and picked Jack up, thought it would be safer for both of us. I don't think it's right getting involved these days. In my youth it would have been a different story, but not these days. The world is a very angry place, or should I say people are far angrier than they used to be?"

"You're not wrong there," Sara agreed. "Were you close enough to overhear any of their conversation?"

"No, and my wife will tell you, my hearing isn't the best, and I refuse to do anything about it."

Sara smiled. "It doesn't matter. What happened next?"

"Like I told the young man earlier when I reported the crime, the two men struck the van owner and threw him in the back of his vehicle then drove off."

"Both men?"

"That's right."

"Are you telling me they left their own van at the park?" Sara asked.

Craig glanced her way and withdrew his phone from his pocket.

"Yes, it was still there when I left the park with Jack. I walked around the block a few times, trying to make sense of it all in my head before I came home and broke the news to Sylvia. She insisted I should ring the station to report the crime. I was in two minds about doing it, but then it struck me watching you on the news bulletin. Do you think this has something to do with the other crimes you're investigating?"

Sara held her phone and scrolled through her photos. She angled it towards Mr Tetley. "Do you recognise this man as one of the two kidnappers?"

"I'm not sure. I was a fair distance away from them. I wouldn't like to lead you up the garden path by saying yes, not when I'm not a hundred percent certain."

"That's perfectly understandable. Can you tell us a little about the van they took off in? Excuse me a second... Craig, ring the station, get a patrol car over to the park, see if the van is still there, and tell them to keep it under observation for now."

Craig dipped out into the hallway to make the call.

"Sorry about that, it's important to implement actions as they come up. Where were we? Ah yes, I asked if you could tell me about the van the kidnappers drove off in."

"It was a green van. When I say green, I don't mean all over, it had some kind of picture on it."

"Can you describe the picture?"

"Not really, otherwise I would have told you that already. I know, it had a lot of writing on the side. Give me a second."

Sara did just that. In the meantime, Craig returned to the room.

"All sorted?" Sara asked.

"Yes, the desk sergeant is going to action it right away."

Mr Tetley thumped a hand on his knee. "I've got it, it was advertising a carpet fitter."

"Did you catch the name?"

"Garners, or could it be Garraways? I'm not convinced either of those is correct, but it was a Hereford number on the side."

Craig removed his phone from his pocket again and scrolled through the internet. "What about Garrison's?"

Mr Tetley beamed at Craig. "You and me, we'd make a great double act. That's the one. It is in Hereford, isn't it?"

"It is," Craig confirmed with a smile.

"That's wonderful," Sara said. "Is there anything else you can tell us?"

"Good grief, haven't I stretched my brain enough to deliver that baby to you?" Mr Tetley chuckled.

"You've done exceptionally well. We're going to shoot off now and get the investigation underway into this man's abduction. Will it be all right if I send a uniformed officer around to see you tomorrow to take down a statement?"

"I'm here most of the time. Can you get them to give me a call first?"

"I'll be sure to do that. Now, please don't worry about what you saw this evening. Like I said earlier, cases like this are few and far between."

"I'll believe you, thousands wouldn't. I hope you find the man safe and well, not like the other victims."

Sara finished off her drink and stood. "We hope so, too. Take care of yourself and your wife."

"I will. I'll show you to the door."

"No, I insist, you stay there, we can find our own way out." Sara smiled.

Craig followed her out of the room.

The moment Sara stepped outside the house, her mobile rang. It was the desk sergeant at the station.

"Evening, ma'am. We've just had an interesting call from a member of the public saying that a greenish van pulled over and dumped some stuff out the back of it."

"Okay, that is interesting. We've been informed by the witness who saw the man being kidnapped a few hours ago that his van was green with a design on the side. You'd better give me the location?"

"In Aylestone Park, in the car park there."

"All right. Have you sent a patrol to the location?"

"They're en route now."

Sara paused to consider the options.

Do I travel to Aylestone Park, see what's been dumped? It's more than likely another body. Or do I head over to where the kidnappers have left the van in the hope that they're on their way back to retrieve it, or even swap vehicles again?

"I'm torn on what to do next. If it's the same van, can we try and pick it up on the ANPRs throughout the city? Should we go to Aylestone, or should I follow my gut and see if the kidnappers return to pick up their vehicle? Help me out here, Craig, what would you do?"

His gaze flitted up and down the road before he responded. "Why don't you go to where the witness saw the man being kidnapped, and I'll shoot over to Aylestone to see how the land lies there...? Er, no, that's a bad idea because it'll mean us splitting up. I couldn't live with myself if anything happened to you after I've made such a naff suggestion."

"Hey, don't worry about me, there's a patrol car at each of the locations. That's right, isn't it, Jeff?"

"Definitely, ma'am. I can always send more at a moment's notice, just say the word."

"Thanks. All right, let's go with your suggestion, Craig. Jeff, can you put an alert out for a van that belongs to a carpet fitter called Danny Garrison? We believe that's the man who these mongrels kidnapped earlier. I'm missing the plate number for his vehicle. Can you source that for me?"

"Leave it with me."

"I'll be in touch if we need extra bodies out here." She ended the call and patted Craig on the back as they returned to their cars. "Good call. Put your foot down to get there. Let me know what you find as soon as you arrive."

Craig nodded, opened the door and slipped inside his car. "Good luck, boss. Can I just add that if the van shows up, please contact me?"

"You'll be the first one I call, I promise. See you later. I've got a good feeling—correction, maybe what I should have said is that I've got a good and bad feeling about this one, Craig. I'm unsure which way it's going to tip, so we need to be ready for every eventuality, agreed?"

"I'm right there with you on that, boss." He started his engine and sped away.

With trepidation gnawing at her gut, Sara got in her vehicle and travelled the short distance to find the patrol car sitting at the top of the road where the park was situated. She pulled over and lowered her window to speak with the driver. Not recognising him, she flashed her ID. "DI Ramsey. You're standing out like a sore thumb. We believe the suspect might be on his way to switch vehicles; we need to be prepared for that. Can I suggest you park around the corner and then hop on board with me? My car's less conspicuous which means we'll be able to get closer to their van without highlighting the fact we're around."

"Great idea. Give me two ticks to dump our car, ma'am."

Sara nodded. The patrol car reversed, and seconds later, two uniformed officers slipped into her back seat.

"Nice evening, gents. I'll pull into the gap over to the right. That'll give us an excellent view of the van and allow us to make a move without too much hassle."

"I agree," the older officer said. "What do we know about the suspect, if anything?"

"Nothing, not really. If it's the same suspect we've been chasing all week, then so far he's proved to be somewhat elusive but has left a trail of devastation in his wake. This is the closest we've been to him since the beginning of the investigation."

"Let's hope he's not doing all this intentionally and giving us the runaround."

"That's a distinct possibility, but it's a chance I'm willing to take. All the kidnappings have taken place in the evening, just like the one earlier. I've just realised the witness who saw the victim being kidnapped said there were two men. It'll be interesting to see how many show up to retrieve the van and also what has been dumped over the other side of the town at Aylestone. Hopefully, I'll hear from my colleague regarding that, soon. I sense things are about to come to a head this evening."

"Female gut intuition speaking, ma'am?" the younger officer said, earning himself a dig in the ribs from the older man.

"That was unnecessary, Salter."

"Don't be too hard on him, he could be right. All through this investigation we've had virtually nothing to go on. I'm wondering why things have suddenly come to a head. Have the dynamics changed between the kidnappers?"

"Maybe one of them didn't approve of what happened during the final hit. Or maybe I'm guilty of talking out of my... backside," the younger officer said.

"More likely to be the latter," the older officer muttered.

Sara suppressed the giggle threatening to break free. "Only time will tell. All we can do is sit and wait. If their intention is to return for the van tonight, I feel sure they must be heading this way after making the detour to Aylestone."

They sat there for another five minutes, watching and waiting.

Sara's mobile rang, startling her. "DI Sara Ramsey."

"It's Craig, boss. You're not going to like this."

"Go on, Craig, we haven't got time for games. What have you got over there?"

"Two dead bodies."

"Two? Fuck, not what I was expecting to hear. Can you identify them?"

"When I did the search for the carpet fitter, a picture of Danny Garrison came up. He was standing next to his vehicle on his Facebook business page. What I'm getting at is, I believe he's one of the victims."

"And the other? Have you checked them for ID?"

"I have. I've also got a Micky Rease here. Umm... I could be wrong, but I think he's the one who was caught on camera at the architect's office."

"Are you sure?" Sara asked, confused.

"Okay, I'm going to put my neck on the line and say yes, that's a positive."

"Jesus, something must have gone wrong with the partnership. We won't know the ins and outs until we make an arrest. Get the pathologist and SOCO organised over there, Craig. I've got two uniformed officers with me here. If he's heading our way, we'll be ready for him."

"I'd say that was a certainty. Want me to give Barry a bell to join you?"

Sara thought over the suggestion for a moment or two. "He doesn't live far from here, does he? Yes, do that. Apprise him of the situation and ask him, don't order him, to join me."

"I'll get on to him now. Knowing Bas the way I do, he'd be gutted if he missed out on the action."

Sara laughed. "You're assuming there will be some *action*."

"Oops, my mistake. Be in touch soon."

Sara ended the call and heaved out a sigh. "Something has turned sour between the kidnappers. I wonder what that might be," she said, more to herself than to the two uniformed officers sitting in the back of her car.

"Who knows with crazed criminals, the type we're having to deal with more and more these days?" the older officer grumbled.

"What are your names?" Sara asked. "Sorry, I should have asked when I arrived, I'm not usually so rude."

"Not a problem, ma'am, you've had enough shit on your mind to deal with. I'm PC Ray Coppell, and this is my partner, PC Wayne Salter."

"And how long have you been on the Force, Ray?"

"I'm celebrating my twenty-fifth year, ma'am."

"That's amazing, I bet you've seen some changes over the years, haven't you?"

"You could say that. The Force isn't what it used to be. No disrespect intended, ma'am."

"You have my permission to speak freely. What are you getting at?"

"I'm not suggesting the obvious, you know, what with you being a female officer and all…"

She smiled. "I should hope not. I've earnt my rank over the years, worked hard, made sacrifices just like my male colleagues."

"I wasn't suggesting you hadn't. What I was getting at is, the powers that be shouldn't have taken the bobbies off the streets. I know that's going back a few years now, but seriously, that signified the decline of the Force in my opinion."

Sara turned in her seat and looked him in the eye. "Seriously?"

He nodded, and a tinge of colour seeped into his puffy cheeks.

"Actually, I'm inclined to agree with you and have often voiced my concerns along those lines during my service, not that it's done any good."

A car pulled up alongside them, and the driver lowered the window.

"Hi, Barry. Dump your car and join us. I think we'll be well equipped now to tackle the bastard, *if* he shows up."

"Be with you in a second or two, there's a gap up ahead."

Barry parked his car and then ran back to sit alongside Sara who introduced the uniformed officers in the back.

"Thanks for coming out tonight, Barry."

"I wouldn't have missed this for the world, boss. I was only watching a mind-numbing documentary on Aldi that Gemma wanted to see."

"Ouch, sounds like I saved you from a torturous evening."

"You did. Has Craig been in touch since he found the bodies?"

"Not heard a word from him since. No idea what's going on if one of the kidnappers has decided to kill off his partner."

"Makes you wonder, doesn't it? Do you think money was involved? It's usually the root of all evil with criminals."

"Possibly. We haven't sussed out what their motive is behind any of the murders, yet. Maybe there was a financial gain to be had somewhere down the line, and one of the men got greedy and decided to bump off the other one."

Something caught Sara's eye in her rear-view mirror. "Heads-up, guys, I think this is it."

They all dipped lower in their seats until the van sped past them and drew to a halt in front of the vehicle that had been abandoned earlier.

"Shouldn't we go over there?" Wayne asked.

"Hush, lad, let the inspector call the shots, got that?" Ray admonished his partner who then muttered an apology.

"Don't worry, Ray, I think in this instance Wayne might be right. As soon as the suspect jumps out of the van, we'll make our move. I'd hate it if he got away again. But we do it quietly. We need to sneak up on him, not go marching over there, all guns a-blazing, shouting the odds to get his attention."

Everyone nodded their agreement, then they sat in silence until the door of the green van opened and a slim man, wearing faded skinny jeans and a black jacket, leapt out and walked towards the abandoned vehicle, not bothering to cast a cautious glance over his shoulder.

"Okay, let's grab the bastard," Sara ordered.

They left Sara's car and closed the doors quietly. Barry and Sara kept to the road, and the uniformed officers dipped around the other side of the kidnapper's van to surprise him from the pavement.

As if sensing something was going on behind him, the suspect turned and shouted, "Shit!" then took off.

Sara hollered for Wayne and Ray to grab him. Ray stuck out a leg as the suspect ran past him, but the crafty criminal jumped to avoid contact.

"Fuck, he's going to get away," Sara grumbled.

"No, he won't. I've got this, boss," Barry assured her. "Why don't you head back to the car and follow?"

"If you're sure. Take Wayne with you, he seems quite agile. I'll pick Ray up on the way through. The more bodies we've got on hand, the better." Sara returned to her car, started the engine and drew up alongside Ray. She flung open the passenger door and watched the three men up ahead motor around the corner. "Hop in, we'll try and head him off."

Ray slid into the passenger seat, and Sara put her foot down.

"Jesus, I thought I'd grab him, but he was too quick for me. Maybe I should consider calling it a day, I'm not getting any younger," Ray apologised.

"Nonsense, he outwitted all of us. Don't be too hard on yourself, Constable."

"There's no need to be kind, ma'am. I should know my limits at my age and I clearly don't."

"Just keep an eye on the road, you probably know this area better than I do. If you're aware of any shortcuts around here, let me know."

"Hard to predict which direction he's going to take."

"Granted. Keep your eyes peeled all the same. The boys are keeping up with him, for now."

The suspect dipped out of sight up ahead of them.

"Shit, I spoke too soon."

"Take a left here. It'll bring you out on Tanners Lane."

"I'm in your hands." She followed the instructions Ray had given her, and suddenly they were mere feet away from the suspect. "See, you do have your uses. Never doubt yourself, Ray, you've got a wealth of experience under your belt. Damn, I haven't got a Taser with me. What weapons have you got?"

"Young Wayne is Taser-trained. He should have considered using it back there. We both screwed up."

"It's probably my fault. I issued an order to approach him quietly."

"Nonsense, it made sense at the time. How did we know he'd have the speed of a blasted cheetah"

"That's true. The boys are right behind us. I'm going to see if I can get close enough to clip the bastard."

"He's going to cotton on to what you're attempting to do. There are a few bins still out up ahead, watch he doesn't tip one into your path."

Sara put her foot over the brake every time they came up to a bin and then squeezed her foot on the accelerator again once they'd passed the offending item. "Maybe he's too scared of getting caught to think about throwing obstacles in our way."

The suspect went to his right, slipping down an alley.

"Bugger, he's more alert than I gave him credit for." She peered in her mirror to see Barry and Wayne following the suspect down the alley.

"Take another left at the top and an immediate right, then you're going to have to put your foot down, ma'am."

"I'll add a siren for good measure, how about that?"

They both laughed.

"Works well for me, he knows we're on his tail. Hopefully the boys will find the extra push to make their move on him."

Sara followed Ray's instructions to the letter and then was forced to slam on the brakes. She stopped the car inches from the suspect's leg. Barry and Wayne had him pinned to the ground. He was struggling to break free. As far as Sara could see, Wayne hadn't needed to use his Taser. She and Ray hopped out of the car and approached the suspect to find Barry reading him his rights.

"Fuck off, you ain't got nothing on me. Let me go or I'm gonna lodge a complaint with your superiors."

"Whatever," Barry said. "We've got you bang to rights, mate."

"Screw you, arsehole."

Once the suspect's hands had been secured with cuffs, Barry and Wayne hoisted him to his feet. He kicked out and, as expected, attempted to wriggle free, but the two officers refused to let him outsmart them again and held firm.

"Get him in the car. We'll head back to the other vehicles. Officers Coppell and Salter, if you take the suspect back to the station, my colleague and I will head over to Aylestone Park, see what the other officer found at that location."

The colour drained from the suspect's face. "I ain't been

near that place. Don't you go pinning anything on me, you arseholes."

He cussed and kicked out at the back of Sara's seat during the journey back to the other vehicles. Barry helped Ray and Wayne load the suspect into the back of the squad car, and then Barry followed Sara across town to the crime scene at Aylestone Park.

"Christ, am I glad to see you guys. What happened?" Craig asked.

"We arrested him. He refused to give us his name," Barry informed him before Sara had a chance to answer.

"How far away are SOCO?" Sara glanced over her shoulder, sensing they weren't far away, or was that wishful thinking on her part?

"They warned me it could take anything up to an hour to get here. I'm fine waiting around, boss, if you want to head home."

"I'll keep him company," Barry quickly added.

Tears welled up in Sara's tired eyes, and weariness hit her like an express train. "You two are the best. I'll take you up on that kind offer. I'll ring the station, tell them to bang the suspect up in a cell for the night. It'll do him good. Maybe it won't, but you get my drift."

"Enjoy the rest of your evening. At least there will be one less serial killer on the loose tonight," Craig said.

"Such a relief to have caught the bastard. I'm dying to hear what went wrong between them. He seems a mouthy git. Maybe he'll surprise us and spill the beans rather than go down the 'no comment' route. I'll head home now. Don't stay out here any longer than is necessary. I know I don't tell you often enough, but I'm proud of you guys, you *never* let me down."

"All part of the job, boss. Drive carefully," Barry said.

"Goodnight, boss," Craig added.

.   .   .

SARA ARRIVED home to find Mark having a cuddle with Misty in the lounge, his head back, resting his eyes. She made him jump when she planted a kiss on his lips.

"Sorry, I didn't realise you were asleep. I spotted Misty massaging you with her paws."

"That's probably what contributed to me falling asleep. You're back early, or are you?"

"It's almost ten. We had an eventful evening. I'm glad to be home."

"Eventful, how?"

"I'll tell you upstairs. I need a drink. Do you want a glass of wine?"

"I'll fetch it and see to Misty. You go up and get changed."

She kissed him again. "You're the best husband ever."

"I bet everyone says that when there's the offer of a glass of wine on the table, or in bed, in our case."

"Idiot. I doubt it, knowing some of the abuse cases that come our way."

"Appalling. Don't get me started on that subject."

Sara left the room and walked slowly up the stairs, her legs objecting with every painful step she took. She was in desperate need of a shower, always felt the same after making a crucial arrest, but her body was far too tired. Instead, she had a quick wash and cleaned her teeth, although the latter task proved to be a mistake when she took the initial sip of her wine.

"Gross."

"What is? I opened a new bottle. I'll see if we've got another one in the cupboard."

"No, the wine is fine, I just wish I hadn't cleaned my teeth before I took a sip."

"Oh, right, yeah, not the brightest idea you've had tonight."

"Luckily, some of the other ideas proved worthy of an award for Police Officer of the Year." She laughed.

"Really? I can't wait to hear about your brave exploits."

He swiftly removed his clothes, and they slid into bed, shared a quick cuddle and snuggled up as Sara recounted what had taken place in the two hours since she'd been out.

"Wow, when you said your evening had been eventful, you weren't kidding. I'm so proud of you."

"Funny that, I said the same to Barry and Craig before I left them. All in a day's work."

"Get out of here, and then some. Look at the extra hours you've put in today, let alone over the weekend, love. I hope your senior officers appreciate the lengths you go to in order to get a serial killer off the streets."

"I doubt it, it's all part of the job to them, sitting behind their desks all working nine to five."

"That's shocking. I feel for you. I appreciate the effort you put in to keep the streets of Hereford safe."

"Thank you, that's all that matters to me. And makes my job worthwhile."

EPILOGUE

*S*ara approached the station the following day, her insides full of cautious apprehension. She hadn't got a clue how her day ahead was going to pan out, questioning the suspect who didn't even have a name. She couldn't remember ever being in this position before in all her time on the Force.

Barry was chosen to join her in the interview room, proud to be considered for the role. Before setting off to tackle the suspect, they ran the name of the other kidnapper, Micky Rease, through the system and came up with a previous record of burglary for him, but linking him to their interviewee proved to be a mammoth task until Craig stumbled across a picture of the two of them together on Facebook, which led them to Saul Jacobs.

Sara felt sure this was going to come as a severe shock to the suspect, and she couldn't wait to see his response.

Barry began the interview and then threw the questioning over to Sara.

"Right, Saul Jacobs, why don't you tell us what you've been up to the past week or so?"

There was a spark of disbelief which quickly turned to hatred in his eyes before a smile pulled his thin, cracked lips apart. "Wouldn't you like to know?"

"Actually, yes. Are you going to reveal all or not? Do you want me to name all the victims we believe you and Micky Rease have killed in the last eight days? Or should we jump ahead to what happened yesterday evening? What drove you to murder your partner?"

"You tell me, you're supposed to be the shit-hot detective around here."

"What my client means is, that he is not inclined to tell you. From now, he will be giving you a two-word answer to all your questions," the duty solicitor, Mr Braddock, said, his gaze never lifting from the notes he was taking.

"Is that so? I would have thought Mr Jacobs would be the talkative type. He appeared to be just that when he was arrested yesterday. Care to tell us why you decided to kill your partner? What went wrong? Was it a difference of opinion about what method of kill you had in mind for your latest victim, Danny Garrison?"

"Might have been." He threw himself backwards and twisted his plastic cup in his hands.

His solicitor leaned in to offer more advice, but he laughed.

"You think you know it all," he said to his solicitor. "She's coming across as having far more nous about her than you."

"Charming. Feel free to find another solicitor to fight your corner." With that, Braddock packed his pad and pen away in his briefcase and left the room to the sound of Jacob's laughter.

"That's not going to help your cause, Saul. Why do that?" Sara said the instant the door slammed behind the solicitor.

"Why not? I'm not the type to take instructions from know-it-alls, it gets mighty tedious."

"You clearly have no intention of holding back, so in your own time, why don't you tell us why you and your partner, Micky Rease, killed Adam Pearse, Bonnie Rogers, Jarvis Zamora and Danny Garrison?"

"Let me think… umm… because we could, will that do you?" He stared at Sara and chortled.

"So you're not denying the murders?"

"Nope, what would be the point?"

"Fair enough. Can you tell me why the victims were chosen?"

"Nope, not really, everything was random. Hey, do you know the address we used where we tortured them before we killed them?"

"Not yet, not unless you're willing to divulge that information during this interview."

He gave them the address, and Sara's heart immediately skipped several beats. It made her wonder what the heck this guy was up to.

Why is he being so open with me? What am I missing here?

Sara excused herself for two minutes, walked into the hallway and rang Craig. "Hi, it's me. He's given us an address. Can you take Marissa and go and check it out for me ASAP?"

"We'll get on it right away, boss."

Sara passed over the details and returned to the interview room to put further questions to what was the turning out to be a very obliging suspect. All was going well until Sara received a call from Craig fifteen minutes later.

She excused herself once more and took the call outside. "Did you find anything?"

"Yes, a room designed to be… I suppose, what can only be described as a torture chamber, and two more bodies."

"Shit. Any IDs on the victims?"

"None that I can see. I'm guessing they've been dead for over a week, but that's pure speculation on my part."

"Double shit! Male or female?"

"Both males. You don't suppose it's the other two guys who have been reported missing lately, do you? I can't for the life of me remember their names."

Sara withdrew her notebook from her pocket and flicked back a few pages. "Ian Chance and Patrick Kellen. Check with MissPers, get them to send over a photo of each of the men for you to make a formal identification, if only for our benefit. Jesus, this guy is winding me up something chronic in there. Not in a bad way, he's leaking us the information bit by bit, but it's his frigging attitude I'm struggling to deal with. Still, that's my problem, not yours. Let's get the bodies identified first."

"Stick with it, boss, you've got this. I'll make the call and get back to you later, if anything comes of it."

"Great. Thanks, Craig."

Sara heaved out a sigh and re-entered the interview room for another battle of wills that turned out to be anything but in the end.

She drew the interview to a close after he gave a full confession. He rose from his seat and had the audacity to try and shake her hand, but the constable stepped in to prevent him touching Sara.

"Sodding arsehole," Sara said. "It's true what they say, it takes all sorts to make up this damn world of ours."

"Ain't that the truth?" Barry agreed.

Craig and Marissa came back an hour later, confirming the identification of the victims. Sara and Barry headed off to deliver the bad news to the victims' families. Sara decided they needed a break on the way back to the station and made a detour to the hospital to visit Carla.

Carla beamed when they walked on to the ward. "Hey, I wasn't expecting to see you today. How are things going with the investigation?"

Sara and Barry both gave Carla a quick kiss then sat in the seats on either side of her bed.

"We cracked it," Sara said. "It proved to be relatively easy come the end. And no, that's not me blowing my own trumpet. Barry will back me up, won't you?"

"I will indeed. A weird fucker. The only thing he hasn't told us so far is what he and his partner's motives were for killing the victims."

"Give him time," Carla said. "Once Sara gets him in the interview room again and starts turning the thumbscrews..."

The three of them laughed. Suddenly, Carla winced and clutched her side.

"Does it hurt...?" Sara held up a hand. "Don't answer that... only when you laugh, right?"

Carla grinned. "Yeah, you've nailed it. I'll tell you something..." She glanced around her and then lowered her voice. "I'm desperate to get out of here. Can you do me a favour and kick up a stink like you usually do in this place, Sara?"

"As if! I'm totally respectful when I visit the hospital. What's the food like?"

"In the main, okay, but I'm sick to death of cottage pie now. I need a good Chinese or Indian takeaway to start healing me from the inside out."

Sara smiled. "What are you like? Have they given you any indication of how long you're going to be in here?"

"At least another week. I dread to think what people used to do before mobiles or tablets were invented."

"Glad you're keeping up with the news. I'll be asking questions when you come out. Keep your spirits up, love. We're all missing you back at the station. Everyone said to say hi and to pass on their best wishes. Is Des visiting you often?"

"Thanks, I appreciate the sentiments. Yeah, he drops in

every evening and stays here for three to four hours. He's had enough of this place as much as I have, though."

"You'll soon be home."

"I've heard it said that it's easier to get out of prison than it is to be discharged from hospital these days... I'm hoping to prove them wrong in the next day or so."

"There's no rush, take your time, and make sure you're well enough to leave. The last thing we need is for you to have a relapse while on duty."

"Hark at you, still as bossy as ever."

"I can vouch for that," Barry threw into the mix.

They all laughed.

"I mean it, take your time, Carla, come back when you're fit enough and not a moment sooner, got that?"

"Yes, boss, you know best."

"Hallelujah, it has only taken a life-saving operation for you to realise that."

THE END

THANK you for reading The Games People Play, Sara and Carla's next adventure can be found here **Revenge Streak**

HAVE you read any of my fast paced other crime thrillers yet? Why not try the first book in the award-winning Justice series Cruel Justice here.

OR THE FIRST book in the spin-off Justice Again series, Gone In Seconds.

. . .

WHY NOT TRY the first book in the DI Sam Cobbs series, set in the beautiful Lake District, To Die For.

PERHAPS YOU'D PREFER to try one of my other police procedural series, the DI Kayli Bright series which begins with The Missing Children.

OR MAYBE YOU'D enjoy the DI Sally Parker series set in Norfolk, Wrong Place.

OR MY GRITTY police procedural starring DI Nelson set in Manchester, Torn Apart.

OR MAYBE YOU'D like to try one of my successful psychological thrillers She's Gone, I KNOW THE TRUTH or Shattered Lives.

KEEP IN TOUCH WITH M A COMLEY

Pick up a FREE novella by signing up to my newsletter today.
https://BookHip.com/WBRTGW

BookBub
www.bookbub.com/authors/m-a-comley

Blog

http://melcomley.blogspot.com

Why not join my special Facebook group to take part in monthly giveaways.

Readers' Group

Made in the USA
Las Vegas, NV
08 October 2023

78782303R00122